INEVITABLE I

A TANNER NOVEL - BOOK 1

REMINGTON KANE

INTRODUCTION

INEVITABLE I – A TANNER NOVEL – BOOK 1

Hired killer, Tanner, escapes from a Mexican prison and goes in search of revenge against the man who was to be his latest target.

Mobster Albert Rossetti thought he was safe after he framed Tanner for drug possession and had him locked away inside a Mexican prison—but Tanner broke out.

Rossetti's made peace with the man who hired Tanner to kill him, and the contract was cancelled, but that means nothing to Tanner, who lives by his own rules.

Tanner is coming for Rossetti, despite the man's hit squad, or the determined and troubled female FBI agent chasing him.

Tanner is coming, Tanner is deadly, and Tanner never fails.

ACKNOWLEDGMENTS

I write for you.

—Remington Kane

1

DO YOU WANT FRIES WITH THAT?

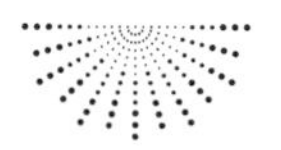

When Tanner saw the crack beneath the door darken, he rolled off the bed while taking the sheets with him, and left the naked hooker to fend for herself.

He fell beside his shotgun, took hold of it, and crawled forward to take aim at the door. It burst open and two guys with guns stood in the threshold, gazing at the hooker.

Tanner fired both barrels of the shotgun, one after another, at an upward angle, hitting the big man in the gut and the short one in the balls. They both let out screams that rivaled the hooker's and slid to the floor of the hotel hallway.

Tanner rushed over, gathered up their weapons and smashed them both in the forehead with the shotgun barrel. The short one raised a hand up to fend off the blow and wound up with four broken fingers besides.

Not that it mattered; they would both bleed out before an ambulance came.

The hooker had stopped screaming and was sitting back against the headboard with her eyes locked on the shotgun.

"I won't hurt you. But don't say shit to the cops."

The blonde said nothing, and Tanner snapped his fingers at her.

"Did you hear me?"

She nodded, causing her breasts to jiggle. "Yes, yes, yes."

Tanner was as naked as she was; however, her body was pale and soft, while his was hard, scarred, and baked brown from the weeks he'd recently spent beneath the Mexican sun. Tanner threw on his jeans, along with a black hoodie and tossed the hooker an extra hundred as he slipped into his boots.

Someone in the hall said, "Holy shit!" and Tanner fired two shots into a corner of the room. The bullets came from the Beretta he had taken from one of Rossetti's thugs, causing the looky-loo and any other nosey types to run back to their rooms.

He didn't know for certain how Rossetti had gotten onto his trail so soon, but he had an idea of how he did it. If he was right, that meant he would soon be going to war with the Conglomerate.

Tanner had reloaded the shotgun and given the room a quick wipe down for prints when the first cop car pulled up out front.

He was on the third floor of the hotel and had to get away before more cops appeared. He had been out of prison for only two days and he sure as hell wasn't going back.

There was a utility closet at the right rear of the hotel, beside it was a laundry chute.

Tanner flipped up the lid and peered down inside a narrow metal tube.

He nodded to himself. He would fit, for he was down to nothing but muscle and gristle.

Tanner was in Brownsville, Texas, inside the Victory Hotel, but he had spent the last ten weeks in a Mexican prison.

Tanner sent the shotgun down first, but only because it couldn't be helped. He needed both hands free. The gun made a muffled sound as it hit bottom and he reasoned that there was a cart full of dirty sheets awaiting him.

Tanner leapt up, grabbed onto a cold-water pipe and slipped his legs into the chute. When he let go of the pipe, he slammed his shoulder against the edge of the chute as he went in. He knew he'd have a beauty of a bruise where it hit.

The chute was tighter than it looked, but it turned out to be a good thing as it slowed his descent. He hit bottom, landing in a cart full of soiled tablecloths, then saw that one of the laundry workers was holding his shotgun. The guy was gawking at it as if it were a piece of alien technology.

The man was a young Asian. The eyes behind his glasses widened in wonder as Tanner slid into view.

Tanner yanked the gun away from the man and shoved him backwards to the floor. When the other workers saw this, they scrambled away to safety, and Tanner headed toward the daylight streaming in from the loading dock.

The laundry was hot and humid and permeated with an odor that smelled like a mixture of soap, steam, and old socks.

Someone had been about to have lunch, because Tanner found a pristine Big Mac sitting in an open carton beside a bag of fries. He scooped up the food, walked out onto the loading dock, and smacked the driver of a linen truck in the back of the head with the butt of the shotgun.

The man groaned, dropped to his knees, and made feeble sounds of protest as Tanner walked through the open rear doors of the truck, past metal shelves and wheeled carts, and slid into the driver's seat.

The keys were in the ignition, and Tanner started the truck and drove off. As he made a hard stop at the exit to let a car pass by, the back doors of the truck slammed shut on their own and Tanner was on his way.

He took his first bite of the Big Mac as he made the left onto a side street, while in the background, a chorus of sirens began.

2
HOLD THE BURKA

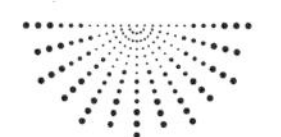

NEW YORK CITY

FBI SPECIAL AGENT SARA BLAKE READ THE MEMO HER boss handed her and smiled.

The SAC, or Special Agent-in-Charge, Martin Brewer, also smiled, while letting his eyes roam over her body. Sara was standing before his desk in a dark, conservative women's business suit. The suit was designed to be conservative, but Sara's body ruined the effect. A burka couldn't hide her curves.

Brewer was fifty-two, old enough to be Sara's father, but not so old that he couldn't appreciate her beauty.

Sara handed back the paper. "So, not only has Tanner escaped prison, but he's back in the States and doing what he does best, killing."

"Yeah," Brewer said, while raising his gaze to meet hers. "However, it appears he killed those two men in self-defense."

"Any ID on the dead men?"

"Oh yeah, they were two hard cases that worked for a thug out there. The local cops say these guys were probably loaned out for a hit, only they were the ones that got hit. I'll email you all the pertinent facts, but right now I want you on a plane for Texas."

"Good, this time I'm coming back with Tanner's scalp. When do I leave?"

"You're to meet Jake Garner at JFK Airport, and there will be a jet waiting."

Sara made a face as she ran a hand through her long dark hair.

"Garner? Really Marty?"

"What's wrong with Jake Garner? He's a hell of an agent."

"Maybe, but he also thinks he's God's gift to women. And he can't go five seconds without staring at my breasts."

Brewer chuckled. "Hell Sara, even I'm guilty of that. You're a beautiful woman, one of my best agents, but still a beautiful woman. Take Garner, he's someone you want at your six when things get heavy."

Sara let out a long breath. Brewer was right. If things went bad, Garner was the agent she'd pick to watch her back. Still, the man could be annoying.

Jake Garner was so good-looking that he couldn't understand why Sara wasn't attracted to him, and he let it be known in subtle and not-so-subtle ways that he wanted her.

Sara wasn't looking to start a relationship, or even have a one-night stand. There was only room for one man in her life and his name was Tanner. Once she dealt with him, then she could think about the future, about starting over, but until she found Tanner and paid him back for what he did to her, the rest of her life was on hold.

"I'll take Garner, hell, I'll work with anyone if it helps me capture Tanner."

"One more thing, the Organized Crime Unit has gotten intel from an informant. There's a mobster in Vegas named Albert Rossetti that wants Tanner dead. It's likely that it was this Rossetti who sent the two thugs after Tanner at that hotel."

"Rossetti? Why does that name sound familiar?"

"Because of Johnny R, the head of the Giacconi Crime Family here in New York. The R stands for Rossetti."

"Is he related to Albert Rossetti?"

"Albert is Johnny's uncle, he moved out to Vegas years ago."

"Why does Albert Rossetti want Tanner dead?"

"The informant didn't know, but he did find out one interesting tidbit. It seems that Tanner was framed on the drug charge that landed him inside that Mexican prison, and it was Rossetti that framed him."

Sara nibbled at her lower lip as she thought things over. "Rossetti must have been Tanner's target when the Mexicans captured him. If so, now that he's free, Tanner will be looking to carry out the contract."

"Still, after all this time?"

"Tanner never gives up until he's fulfilled his contract."

Brewer tapped his desk with a fist. "We tried to get him transferred back here to face murder charges, but the Mexicans kept delaying because all our evidence was based on supposition, and now it's too late."

"We should have two agents from Vegas watch Rossetti. It will help to know where he is at all times."

"Why should we keep tabs on him?"

"Because he's Tanner's next target and you can be sure that the bastard will go after him."

3
AND A BOTTLE OF RUM

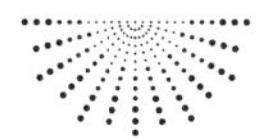

TANNER WANTED TO KILL ROSSETTI AS SOON AS POSSIBLE, but Rossetti would have to wait.

Tanner's priority was to get transportation and money. He was on the prowl for both when he spotted a pimp backhanding one of his girls.

The pimp was white, his bodyguard black, and the girl was a child. Although, Tanner had to admit, with the makeup and high heels the girl could pass for thirteen.

The girl nodded in acquiescence and trod back toward her corner to search for more strangers to pleasure, as the pimp climbed in the back of his silver Mercedes. The bodyguard took the wheel.

Tanner followed. He was still driving the linen truck but knew he had to ditch it soon or else deal with the cops. He had already wiped the linen truck down, erasing his prints, and was wearing a pair of brown cotton gloves that had been lying atop the dashboard.

Tanner watched the pimp's car make a right and head down an alley. When he drove past it, he saw that there was already a guy there in a yellow Honda Civic. He only caught a glimpse of the man, but the dude had drug dealer written all over him.

Tanner pulled the truck to the curb, stuck the shotgun down inside an empty pillowcase and headed to the alley on foot. He knew that all he had on his side was the element of surprise; he intended to use it to its fullest advantage.

Tanner scooped up an old rum bottle from the gutter and, without looking, tossed it hard and high down the alleyway.

The bottle spun end over end and smashed apart against the back wall, showering the three men with broken glass while making them instinctively look in that direction.

By the time they realized that Tanner was running toward them, he was close enough to use the shotgun. He fired one barrel at the bodyguard and shredded the man's face. The bodyguard fell to the ground screaming, while the drug dealer, a punky-looking dude with blond cornrows, reached under his Cowboys jersey for a gun.

Tanner blasted him in the chest and he fell against the pimp and dragged the man to the ground, where they both settled beside the screaming bodyguard.

The pimp went for the automatic that his bodyguard had dropped. Tanner gripped the shotgun like a bat and swung for a home run. It would have likely only been a triple, but it killed the pimp all the same. The bodyguard was next and after two hard whacks with the shotgun, the man stopped his screaming.

Tanner didn't know if the drug dealer was dead or not, but the man felt limp when he kicked him in the ribs. After patting him down, Tanner came away with a bag of coke, six hundred in cash and a Ruger, while the pimp had over five grand in small bills.

The keys were still in the Mercedes and Tanner backed it out of the alley, rolling over the pimp's legs in the process, then headed for the highway.

4
STRAIGHT OUT OF HELL

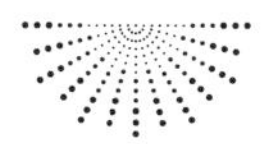

In Las Vegas, Albert Rossetti looked at his right-hand man, Ramone, with disgust.

Rossetti sat behind his desk in a special chair big enough to hold his bulk.

"He killed them both?"

"Yeah."

"You said he would, I know. All right, send Aldo and his crew."

"Four men?"

"What? Four's not enough? Who do you think this guy is? Rambo?"

"No, Tanner is more dangerous."

"Hell, I figured the Mexicans would keep him locked up for life. How the hell did he get out?"

Ramone took a seat on the corner of the desk. He was a slim man with a dusky complexion and dead eyes. When he moved, it was always with grace.

"I don't know, but four men won't do it. He'll keep coming, and unless he's stopped he'll kill both of us."

"Put out the word, five G's to whoever bags him, and that includes Aldo and his boys."

Ramone nodded in agreement. "That's a start, but ten G's and a thousand-dollar finder's fee would bring out the hustlers and make Tanner's life miserable."

Rossetti thought about that for a moment, then searched Ramone's eyes.

"This Tanner, do you think he'll make it to Vegas?"

"I do. It's why I'm not going after him. If I have to face him, I'd rather do it on home turf."

Rossetti ran the back of his hand against the graying stubble of his fat face.

"Aldo will kill him. Him and his boys took out that Jamaican crew singlehandedly last year, and they were outnumbered three-to-one."

"Tanner's not Jamaican."

"Where's he from?"

Ramone's lips curled in a sneer.

"Tanner came straight out of hell."

As Tanner drove along US 77 headed north, he thought about the events that had landed him inside a Mexican prison.

Tanner was a hit man, a hired killer, or as he liked to think of himself, a trained assassin. He had never failed at an assignment.

A member of the Conglomerate had hired him. The Conglomerate was an alliance between the criminal underworld and certain corporate empires.

As the world became a global marketplace, traditional Western corporate tactics and practices were revealed to be ineffective in some sectors of the world.

Dictators and warlords weren't dissuaded from committing blatant acts of theft because they were threatened with legal action, and would sometimes confiscate whole industries in the guise of nationalization.

In earlier times, Western governments would step in and remedy situations with embargoes or the withholding of foreign aid. However, those threats grew less ominous over time and the government often demanded more for their aid than would have been lost without it.

Enter the Conglomerate, a partnership formed to protect corporate profit across the world, by fighting fire with napalm. The Mafia and other organized crime factors became aligned with big business and would act as their enforcers.

While a Harvard Business School graduate might not know how to deal with thugs and extortionists, his criminal partners certainly did, and would do so, ensuring that the profit pipeline kept flowing.

Frank Richards, a corporate member of the Conglomerate, hired Tanner to kill Albert Rossetti, because Rossetti had been holding back a percentage of the take of his illegal activities.

In the old system, organized crime would bleed a business dry by demanding ever increasing "protection payments." Under the new system, though, everyone contributed a percentage of their income.

No casino control commission in the world would allow a man like Albert Rossetti to have ownership of a casino. However, he could profit from one owned by a corporation he was aligned with, by acting as that entity's strong-arm enforcer and running the hooker and drug trade.

Also, if needed, a respectable corporate member could provide an alibi, while a messy and expensive divorce could simply evaporate when an executive's estranged spouse suffered an "accident."

Rossetti was part of the Conglomerate in Vegas and hid behind the facade of respectability his corporate partners enjoyed, to the enrichment of both.

Tanner had been paid well to get the job done and paid up front in full, it was the only way he worked. His reputation was such that once money changed hands, you knew the target was dead.

Rossetti discovered that it was Tanner who was coming after him when a friend of Tanner's betrayed him.

Tanner would deal with that turncoat all in good time, but the main thing on his mind was killing Rossetti.

He had been paid to perform a service and he would do so or die trying. Tanner didn't believe in much at all, but he believed in himself. Once he took a job, he would carry it out regardless of time or travail.

Rossetti arranged for Tanner to be driving a vehicle that had drugs hidden in its trunk, then he tipped off the Mexican authorities.

After rounding a curve on Route 281 in Mexico, Tanner found himself facing ten soldiers, and minutes later they "discovered" the heroin in the car.

After a joke of a trial, Tanner was thrown in prison and put to work at hard labor on a building project, which was located on the outskirts of the Mexican city of Matamoros.

Each day the guards would work him and the other prisoners hard for long hours in the hot sun, and Tanner kept his head down and waited for his chance to break free.

In the weeks he was there, he saw two failed attempts at escape and learned from each one what not to do.

As time passed and the building project neared

completion, he thought he might have to take a chance on a desperate move, or else risk being locked behind prison walls forever, or perhaps killed.

He'd been cornered by a pair of fellow inmates just days before he escaped. The men had come at him with makeshift blades, as a guard looked the other way.

They were on the work detail at the construction site and Tanner held them off by brandishing a hammer. The conflict ended when another guard came over, but Tanner watched his back even more than usual after that incident.

He had no idea why the men came after him, but he thought that maybe they were paid by Rossetti to kill him.

The construction site was difficult to escape from, but the prison would no doubt have proven to be impossible to leave. Many had tried and never even made it past the first of three razor wire fences.

Then, two days ago, a group of prisoners stabbed a guard and took his rifle. One of the group proved to be a talented marksman and killed two other guards before he was shot in the hip and disabled. Another inmate grabbed the rifle and began shooting, but all his shots were either high or wide and he was killed.

That last bit Tanner had watched take place through the rearview mirror of a jeep he'd stolen while the guards were fighting off the other escapees. Three bullets slammed into the jeep, but none of the shots was harmful to the vehicle's performance and Tanner made it into Matamoros, where he ditched the jeep and hid out in a vacant apartment.

He traveled by night through the desert and crossed the border into Texas like a thief.

After robbing a two-bit pot dealer and taking the man's wallet, weed, cell phone, and shotgun, Tanner had a steak dinner, bought a bottle of wine, and hired a hooker.

He had been enjoying his freedom, but then the two thugs appeared and it was time to go on the run again.

However, Tanner was done with hiding. He had a job to do. He had been hired to kill Albert Rossetti and killing the bastard was exactly what he was going to do.

It was inevitable. He was inevitable, as inevitable as death.

Tanner turned his vehicle onto I-37 North, pressed down hard on the gas, and headed for Vegas.

5
YOUR AVERAGE PORN STAR

Lillian Sorrell watched her husband, Dwight, pace about their home office. They lived in a ranch-style house in Spring Valley, Nevada, near Las Vegas.

Something was seriously wrong, Lillian could tell, but she couldn't get Dwight to open up to her. She decided to try again, walked over, and fell into his arms.

"Talk to me," she said. She was thirty, a brunette, with large blue eyes and long legs. Lillian had once been a showgirl, but she gave it up to become an RN and was now working toward a medical degree.

Dwight was in commercial real estate, had been for years, but until recently, it had been only one of his occupations. His second business endeavor had been on the darker side of things. He had worked with Tanner as a go-between for clients.

When Rossetti learned that Tanner had been hired to kill him, he had kidnapped Lillian and forced Dwight to turn on his friend. Dwight Sorrell traded Tanner for his wife's safety while knowing that Tanner would not forgive the betrayal.

Lillian had known nothing about her husband's underworld connections but agreed to stay with Dwight if he retired from that side of things. Dwight did so, while thinking that Tanner would spend his remaining years rotting away in Mexico. Dwight prayed that no others would come after him.

Although he was Tanner's go-between for clients, Dwight rarely had knowledge of who the targets were. He was simply a middleman who passed on information from other sources, and those other sources handed over their information in sealed envelopes, such as the one he received that morning. Until that envelope arrived, Dwight had thought that Tanner was still in Mexico.

But Tanner was out, Tanner was coming, and Dwight knew he was a dead man.

Dwight stared back at Lillian. He was a tall, handsome man who had come from a good family and been pulled into criminal activities by an ex-girlfriend. The girlfriend didn't last, but the lure of easy money did. As one thing led to another, he found himself working for various criminals.

Tanner had been one of his clients and he had known the man through the ex-girlfriend, who had occasionally worked for Tanner as a spotter for targets.

Dwight and Tanner became friends, of a sort, given Tanner's innate inimical nature. Dwight believed it was because Tanner thought of him as someone non-threatening, but in the end, Dwight had proven nearly lethal.

Rossetti had wanted Dwight to kill Tanner outright by sneaking up on him and blowing his brains out. Dwight told the man he could never do it, and suggested setting Tanner up for the drug bust instead.

Rossetti agreed to the plan, Dwight planted the drugs, and when Tanner drove toward Rossetti's supposed location in Mexico, it was Dwight who made certain Tanner was arrested.

"Tanner broke out of prison," Dwight told his wife, and then waited to let the implications of those words sink in. It didn't take long.

Lillian got a horrified look on her face and began pacing as her husband had done earlier.

"We have to run, hide somewhere."

Dwight hung his head. "No, that would just put you in danger. Tanner would find us, and you might get killed along with me."

"I don't care. I'm not leaving you."

"I want you to go to your mother's while I stay here and face him, but with any luck, Rossetti will kill him before he gets to me."

"I'll go to my mother's, so you don't have to worry about me, but then I want you to hide somewhere too."

Dwight shook his head. "No, because then Tanner might find you first and use you to lure me into the open. You can run from Tanner, but you can't hide from the man. I knew that when I helped to frame him, but I was between a rock and a hard place, and I thought I could outsmart him. I was wrong and now I'm about to pay for it."

Lillian hugged him again, as she pressed her face against his chest.

"Rossetti will stop him. Rossetti will stop Tanner and then you'll be safe."

Dwight kissed the top of his wife's head, knowing that Tanner would not be stopped, and that a showdown was imminent.

SARA LEFT THE CORONER'S OFFICE IN THE HOSPITAL basement where the dead pimp was, with Special Agent Jake Garner following behind her down the hallway.

She could feel Garner's eyes on her. The man wanted her and made no pretense otherwise. She assumed he thought his attention was flattering, but Sara just thought the man was a pig.

As they stepped onto the elevator, Garner stood beside her. He was a handsome man whose lips curved in a perpetual smile, as if life were one big party, as if sorrow didn't exist. He had dark hair, dark eyes, and his track record with women rivaled that of your average porn star.

Women flowed toward Garner the way the surf moved toward the shore. Sara was one of the rare ones that resisted his charms and she assumed Garner thought she would give in to him someday, and that it was just a matter of time.

"Does that look like Tanner's work?" Garner asked her.

"Yes, but the linen truck cinches it, even if he did wipe it for prints. Tanner likely killed them for their weapons, vehicle, and money. By now, he's probably dumped the Mercedes and moved on to something else."

"Why don't we just head to Vegas and stay near Rossetti? If that's where Tanner is headed, then that's where we should be."

Sara nodded in agreement. "You're right, but I was hoping to intercept him."

"So, Sara, just how rich are you?"

She gave him a startled look. "What do you mean?"

"That's a designer suit you're wearing, and unless you're on the take or have a sugar daddy, you've got some bucks. Hell, those shoes alone cost nearly a grand."

Sara smirked at him. "You seem to know a lot about women's fashion."

"No, I just know women."

The elevator reached the lobby. When they stepped off, Sara noticed the other women nearby gazing at Garner as if he were a movie star.

As they walked past the reception desk, the young woman that had greeted them on their arrival called Garner over and pressed something into his hand. They then exchanged a few words, and Sara saw the woman pout in disappointment.

Garner smiled at the receptionist and stuck the object she'd given him into his pocket.

Once they were back in their rental, Sara asked a question.

"Did that woman give you her phone number?"

"Yes."

"And why the sad look?"

"I explained to her that I wouldn't be in town long enough to hook up."

"But you're keeping her number, just in case?"

"That's right, and she also gave me a souvenir to remember her by."

"What souvenir?"

Garner reached into his pocket and took out the pair of panties the girl had given him, with her number written in black magic marker atop the red lace.

Sara made a face of disgust, started the car, and drove toward the airport, as Garner tucked the panties away for safekeeping.

6
THOSE MEDDLING KIDS

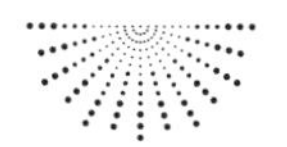

TANNER STOPPED FOR THE NIGHT AT A CRAPPY MOTEL outside Las Cruces, New Mexico.

The place was an absolute shithole, but it would do for the night and there was only one other car parked in the lot.

The desk clerk was drunk and getting drunker, but he accepted Tanner's cash with a smile and went back to watching a ball game.

Normally, Tanner would have driven straight to Vegas to do the deed he was hired to do. But ten weeks of hard, backbreaking labor under the hot Mexican sun, while subsisting on prison rations, had left him in less than peak condition. He decided to grab some sleep before moving on.

He woke early, at first light. The night before, he had dumped the pimp's Mercedes in the parking lot of a diner a mile away, before walking back to the motel.

He needed to get his hands on another car before the other guests stirred, because it was their car he planned to steal.

He could tell by the sounds coming through the thin walls that they were a couple, an energetic couple, judging by the hours of on-again, off-again sex they had engaged in.

Tanner was about to leave after wiping down the room, when he heard a vehicle roll to a stop outside his door, even though the driver had cut the engine.

Tanner peeked past an outer edge of the curtain on the room's only window and watched as three men exited a large, white pickup truck, while leaving their doors open to aid in a quick exit.

The men were all heavyset, but also had the look of hard men. They each wore faded jeans with denim jackets and boots. One of them was sporting a cowboy hat.

The fattest of the three nodded toward the motel and took a gun out of a shoulder holster. The gun was big, a Desert Eagle. Tanner knew he had to take the fight to them while they still believed he was asleep.

Tanner stuck the Ruger he'd taken off the drug dealer in his side pocket and an automatic that had belonged to the pimp's bodyguard, he tucked behind his back.

With the shotgun pressed against his shoulder, he ripped open the door to his room and fired one barrel. Tanner watched bright blue eyes widen on the face of the fat man with the Desert Eagle an instant before his shotgun pellets obliterated them and turned the man's head to red mist.

To Tanner's shock, the door to the room beside his had been kicked in while he was opening his own door, and the man with the cowboy hat was nowhere in sight. A scream came from the room, followed by a gunshot, but Tanner only took note of these things peripherally, because he was too busy emptying the second shotgun shell into the third man.

The man fell atop his fat friend's corpse, where he moaned, thrashed about, and died. Tanner dropped the empty shotgun and grabbed up the Desert Eagle. Cowboy hat came stumbling out of the other room, while struggling with a kid in blue boxer shorts for possession of a gun.

The gun went off again and flattened a tire on the couple's car, but the fresh-faced kid was doing his damnedest to wrest it away.

A topless girl in pink lace panties appeared in the doorway saying, "Be careful, Billy!" When she spotted Tanner, she shrieked and covered herself with her arms. "Please don't kill us, mister. Ricky getting hurt was an accident. I swear it."

Tanner didn't know what she was talking about and didn't care; he just knew he had to leave before the cops came.

He fired the Desert Eagle once into the side of the man in the cowboy hat and watched as the exit wound exploded in a shower of gore.

After retrieving his shotgun, Tanner headed for the white pickup truck.

The boy called to him. The kid was barely out of his teens and had dark hair and curious green eyes.

"Why did you help us?"

Tanner smirked. "Help? I'm pretty sure I killed all three of them, kid."

The girl came out of the room while shrugging on a flower print dress and tossed the boy his clothing. When she looked at the flat tire and the dead men, her face collapsed, and she cried.

The kid went to her. "It's all right, Cindy, we're safe."

Tanner looked around. The interstate was too far away for anyone to have seen or heard anything, but the desk clerk was likely calling the cops.

As Tanner settled behind the wheel of the pickup, the kid called to him.

"Hey! Take us with you, please?"

Tanner opened his mouth to tell the kid to go to hell, but then realized that they would make good cover when he entered Vegas.

Rossetti's men would be looking for a man on his own, not a trio.

"Get in," Tanner said, as he started the truck. Afterwards, he tossed out the half can of beer that was sitting in the cup holder.

When the girl disappeared back into the room, he nearly took off, but she emerged just seconds later with a duffel bag and ran toward them with her long blonde hair trailing behind her. Tanner told her to toss the bag in the bed of the truck, and off they went.

As he drove by the motel office, he saw that the clerk was asleep in a chair with a beer bottle still gripped in his hand.

When the man woke, he'd have an interesting day.

Tanner headed for the highway, for Vegas, and for revenge.

7
DUMB AND DUMBER

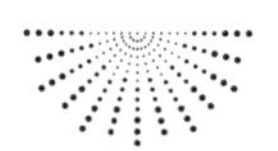

Earl and Merle Carter were sitting at a booth inside Pogo's bar in Vegas and talking excitedly about the price on Tanner's head.

Ten grand was huge money to their way of thinking, and although they had never killed anyone, they had hurt people for far less money, as they traveled through life trying to escape the hand fate had given them.

Neither of them was very bright, nor good-looking, or personable. They weren't blessed with any discernible talents, and other than a long-lost half-sister, all they basically had was each other.

The Carter boys did have one thing going for them, though, animal cunning, and that plus an unending desire to be rich, was what powered them through their empty and meaningless lives.

They looked out the window at the activity taking place in front of the pool hall, where Rossetti's men were gathering to go after Tanner.

"That big guy in the suit is named Aldo," Merle said. Merle was five-foot-eight and scrawny, with a long face, thin lips and dull gray eyes. His brother Earl was a carbon copy of him, except for the color of his hair. Merle's hair was dark brown, while Earl's was two shades lighter.

They weren't twins, but they were born the same year. Merle popped out of his mother's womb on a bitter January day and Earl followed on a similar day the following December.

Earl leaned across the table. "You think Aldo will lead us to Tanner, but so what? That just means we'll get to see him kill Tanner."

"Maybe, but I hear this Tanner is a badass. Maybe he'll get a chance to run from Aldo and his boys and straight toward us, wounded and ripe for the pluckin'. Anyway, Aldo will have more luck findin' him. I have no idea where to look for him, do you?"

Earl leaned back in his seat. "Hell, he could be anywhere for all I know, so yeah, we'll tail Aldo and his boys and hopefully get a shot at Tanner."

Merle reached across the table and punched his younger brother playfully on the shoulder.

"We're gonna get that money and then it's party time."

Earl grinned back at him, for like his brother, he had no real clue who they were going after. But they would learn, and the lesson would be a bitter one.

SARA AND GARNER WERE IN THE FBI'S LAS VEGAS Division awaiting word on Tanner.

Sara stared at Garner and wondered when the man slept. She had seen him disappear into his hotel room in the company of two blonde sisters he'd met in the casino, and both women looked tired and, Sara had to admit, sated, as they left his hotel room early that morning.

Sara had been about to knock on Garner's door to hassle him and tell him to get his shit in gear, when the man opened the door, fully dressed in a charcoal-hued suit, and smiled at her from a freshly shaved face.

"I'm ready when you are, partner," Garner said, and the way he said it, as his eyes roamed over Sara, she knew he meant he was ready for more than just work.

She had ignored the double entendre and headed for the elevator.

"Special Agent Blake?"

Sara broke free of her memories and turned to face an agent named Whitman. Whitman was twenty-three and a rookie, but Sara thought the man seemed professional.

"Has something happened?" Sara asked, as both she and Garner rose to their feet, ready to move.

"Yes ma'am, our two agents in the field are reporting that several of Rossetti's men are heading out of Vegas and that there are now rumors that Rossetti's placed a price of ten grand on Tanner's scalp."

Garner whistled softly. "That kind of money will bring out any hood with a gun."

Sara thought for a moment before speaking.

"We'll wait here. If Rossetti's men or anyone else bags Tanner we'll hear of it, and if he makes it to Vegas, then we'll be here and ready for him."

The agent excused himself and Sara and Garner sat down again.

Garner stared at her, and for once, he was looking into her eyes.

"You want this Tanner badly, don't you?"

"Marty spoke to you, didn't he?"

"Yeah, he said you had a reason for wanting to see Tanner brought down, but he didn't say what it was."

"Just know one thing, Garner."

"What's that?"

"I'll do my job and try to bring Tanner in so that we can question him and gather info on the people who have hired him, but if he resists at all, I'll kill Tanner. A smart man wouldn't get in my way."

"I hear you, Sara, and I've got your back."

Sara smiled at him. "Thanks, Jake; it's nice to know you're not a total jerk."

Garner smiled back at her. "Nobody's perfect."

8
IT'S JUST TANNER

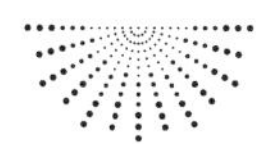

As Tanner drove along, Billy and Cindy told him their story.

They had both lived on a ranch in Colorado that was bigger than most towns. Billy was a drifter who hired on as a ranch hand, while Cindy's family had worked on the ranch for generations.

The owner of the ranch was a man named Hank O'Grady, and Hank's only son, Ricky, had become obsessed with Cindy.

Cindy never liked Ricky much, because he was spoiled and had knocked up a friend of hers when the girl was fourteen and Ricky was eighteen. Cindy's friend had an abortion and her family moved off the ranch, while Ricky went off to some fancy college.

When he returned to the ranch to stay, he went after Cindy, practically stalking her, while threatening to have her father, the ranch foreman, fired.

Meanwhile, Cindy had fallen in love with Billy, a fact that Ricky ignored. Eventually, the two boys fought, and

Cindy claimed that Ricky fell on his own knife, but Tanner suspected that maybe Billy helped him to fall on it. In any event, they were on the run.

"Ricky's dead?" Tanner asked.

"No. Billy and I took him to the ranch infirmary, and they said he'd be fine, but we ran anyway, because Mr. O'Grady would have had Billy hauled off to jail, or probably worse."

"So, what's your plan?" Tanner asked.

"We were going to Mexico," Billy said. "But then we figured we'd go to Vegas and hide there until things died down some. Cindy has always wanted to see the Grand Canyon, so we'll go there soon too."

The three of them sat together in the front seat, as the pickup truck's back seat was so cramped that it could cripple a midget.

The young and tasty Cindy was seated beside Tanner, with Billy to her right, and Tanner could feel himself growing aroused. The whore in Brownsville had taken the edge off, but after having been locked away for months, he needed more than a little time spent with one woman.

Cindy had been eyeing him now and then. At first, Tanner thought it was sexual interest, but then he realized it was just fascination with him because he had killed three men.

She was wary of him, which made her wiser than Billy, who accepted him as a friend right away.

Not very smart of Billy, Tanner thought.

There were men out there who would kill Billy to get to Cindy, either to rape her, or to sell her to white slavers for a tidy profit.

Tanner had never been into either activity, but if he had been, he would have murdered Billy upon meeting him. Then Cindy would have been his, to do with as he pleased.

The road curved right and the slight centrifugal force made Cindy lean against Tanner. He felt her softness, smelled her scent and felt himself stir.

As soon as Rossetti was dead, Tanner planned to head somewhere tropical and bang the crap out of anything hot, blonde, and female.

"Mr. Tanner," Cindy said.

"It's just Tanner."

"Oh, okay. Thank you for helping us, Tanner, and we can pay for the gas and food along the way."

Tanner would have preferred it if Cindy repaid him with her body, but he kept that desire to himself.

"I actually thought those men had come for me. There's a man named Rossetti that wants me dead."

"Why does he want to kill you?" Cindy asked.

"Self-preservation, he's trying to kill me before I can kill him."

Cindy's eyes widened. "Oh."

"This O'Grady, he sent men after you instead of the law, so I guess that means he's a mobster of some kind?"

Billy nodded. "He's not fully legit. He owns a whorehouse and probably deals in weed too, but he ain't connected or nothing like that; he just owns a lot of things… and people."

"He owns my daddy," Cindy said, while making a face. "Daddy was trying to get me and Ricky together. He said we'd be set for life if Ricky married me, never mind what I want."

"But O'Grady will send more men after you, right?"

"Yeah, if they can find us," Billy said.

"He sent three the first time, so he'll probably send more?"

"I guess. O'Grady runs the county and he's got hundreds of men working for him."

Tanner thought about that and a plan formed in his mind, a plan that might help him kill Rossetti.

9

THE 90 POUND LOT LIZARD

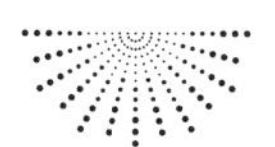

WHEN SARA LEARNED THAT A MAN FITTING TANNER'S description was a suspect in a multiple homicide at a New Mexico motel, in her mind, it reaffirmed the fact that Tanner was headed toward Vegas.

However, when she learned that the dead men were all employees of a Colorado rancher named Hank O'Grady, she became confused.

She then talked to an FBI agent in Colorado who provided her and Garner with background on Hank O'Grady. That same agent said that he would get back to them with more detail once he talked to a friend who worked on O'Grady's ranch.

"It sounds like Tanner has stumbled into more trouble," Garner observed.

"Those men could have been after the reward money Rossetti's placed on Tanner's head, but it's not likely, since they were from Colorado. The desk clerk at the motel said there was a young couple staying there too, and the car they left behind had Colorado plates. It was registered to a William Benton, age twenty."

"Then it sounds like Tanner could be driving a car with Colorado plates if he took the dead men's ride," Garner said.

"Yeah, but I wouldn't bother looking for them, I'm sure that by now he's switched the plates out."

~

Sara was correct, because Tanner, along with Cindy and Billy, was inside a diner off I-10, north of Phoenix, Arizona.

He had already replaced the Colorado plates for a different set he'd taken off another pickup truck, but held on to the Colorado plates, which he figured he could use later.

The diner was full of truckers, because it was part of a truck stop that offered diesel engine repair and a truck wash.

Every man in the place eyed Cindy with lust in their eyes, but they'd take one look at Tanner and keep their distance.

After eating a large breakfast, Tanner told the kids it was time to get back on the road.

As Tanner pulled out of the exit and onto the highway, he hadn't noticed the woman watching him from the cab of a big rig, a woman that knew him. She also knew that there was a price on his head.

~

Two years ago, Tina had been one of the best pieces of ass that money could buy.

She'd been a high-priced call girl then, working out of Las Vegas, and many men had paid upwards of five grand a night to sleep with her. But that was before she became a meth addict.

Now, she was a ninety-pound lot lizard, with scabs on her lined face. She traveled around to different truck stops giving blow jobs for twenty a pop, no pun intended.

She had just raised her head up from the lap of a black trucker who stank of cheap cigars, when she spotted Tanner walking toward the pickup.

Tina studied Tanner while swallowing the trucker's load, no pun intended, again. The man had paid ten dollars extra for the service and a stick of gum would mask the taste later.

It was Tanner she was seeing, Tina was sure of it, although the man looked thinner and darker than she remembered him being. And Tina did remember him, as a smile crossed her wet lips.

She'd been comped to Tanner on several occasions and he had been one of her favorite clients, because the man actually knew how to fuck. She'd even come once or twice with Tanner, a rare event for her.

Still, Tina couldn't say she ever liked him. Tanner was a cold man, not cruel, and he never hurt her the way some men had, but she knew that she had been something to fuck for Tanner, and nothing else.

There had never been a hint of cuddling after sex, no sense of affection and, thank heaven, the man never asked her how she became a hooker, as so many others had over the years.

As Tanner drove out of the lot, Tina kept repeating his license plate number to herself until she had it memorized. Afterwards, she climbed down from the rig and went inside the ladies' room of the diner, where she sat in a stall. After removing the gum from her mouth, she made a call.

"Hey Eddie, it's me Tina. Yeah, yeah, how's tricks?

That one never gets old, Eddie. Now listen, isn't there a finder's fee for spotting that guy Tanner?"

There was a pause on the line, then Tina heard Eddie shouting a question at someone. When he spoke to Tina again, he told her there was a thousand dollar finder's fee to anyone who knew where to find Tanner.

Tina's hand trembled as she held the phone. With that much money, she could keep herself in crystal for weeks without having to suck one dick.

She told Eddie what she knew and said she'd hitch a ride to Vegas to collect her money. She tried not to think about what would happen to Tanner because of her, even though she could guess why Rossetti was looking for him. No, all Tina was thinking about was her next hit of ice, but then, that's what made her an addict.

ALDO LEARNED OF TINA'S TIP AN HOUR LATER, WHEN Ramone called and gave him the details.

Ramone had also passed orders down through their network of dealers that they'd pay a grand to anyone who spotted Tanner's pickup and kept it in sight. They didn't have people in Arizona, but they knew people there and Ramone told Aldo to be on standby near the border, and wait for Tanner to enter the state.

Aldo agreed, and he and his men were inside a coffee shop in Boulder City, Nevada, just waiting for news.

Aldo was forty and had been a thug for hire since high school, when he would help his old man shake down late payers for a loan shark. He had large hands with prominent veins and a naturally mean face, and although he didn't get off on hurting people, he also didn't mind doing it either.

He had no fear of Tanner, despite Ramone's warning that the man was a hard case. Aldo knew Tanner was a hit man and he thought that such men were all punks who would rather shoot you from the shadows than face you head-on.

To Aldo, Tanner was just another jerk who needed planting out in the desert. He was already thinking about how he would spend the bonus.

Aldo looked over at his three men, saw that they all looked relaxed, and knew they considered Tanner an easy kill, just as he did. Once Tanner was spotted, they'd run him down, whack him, take a picture of the corpse as proof, and then plant him.

The planting would be the hardest part of the whole thing, but that was his men's problem. Aldo didn't dig graves anymore; he only made sure that there was something to toss in them.

He leaned back in his seat and took a sip of coffee, while thinking that the day would be a good one.

He couldn't have been further from the truth.

10
CALL ME RAMONE

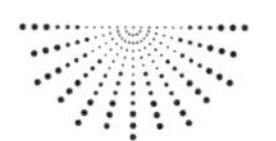

EARL AND MERLE CARTER SAT IN A STOLEN CHEVY IMPALA, while taking turns watching Aldo and his men through a pair of binoculars.

Earl had gone inside a nearby donut shop and gotten coffee, and now they were waiting for Aldo to make his next move.

While Earl was gone, Merle had called a blackjack dealer he knew that sold a little pot on the side, and the word on the street was that Tanner was headed their way in a white pickup.

Merle figured that Aldo must be waiting for someone to spot Tanner and call in his location. That was good. It meant that things were moving along and that maybe they'd be over by the end of the day.

But Merle had learned something else, had gained more knowledge about Tanner's rep, and if what he heard was true, it made him nervous.

He filled his brother in on what he had learned and waited for his take on things.

Earl gave a shrug. “There’s two of us. We can handle Tanner if we’re careful.”

“They say that the dude has killed a lot of people, so we’d better watch our asses around him.”

“Yeah, but first he’s got to get past Aldo and his boys.”

“The dude broke out of prison. He’ll slip away from Aldo and then we’ll surprise him, but I ain’t dyin’ for ten G’s.”

Earl stared at his older brother. “You’re scared of Tanner, ain’t you?”

Merle broke eye contact and went back to watching Aldo. After nearly a minute passed, he spoke.

“Remember Johnny Cato?”

“Yeah, the foreign dude who tried to muscle Bo Manderelli and take his turf in Florida. That was about three years ago, right?”

“Right, and after screwin’ that up, him and his men went to Jersey to try to muscle in there. There were sixteen of them, Earl, sixteen stone cold killers. Manderelli hired this guy Tanner to kill Johnny Cato and said he’d pay an extra three grand for every one of Cato’s men. Tanner killed them all in one night. It wasn’t until the maids smelled the rot of the bodies that anyone even knew it had happened.”

“Sixteen dudes at once, how?”

“He got them in their sleep with a silenced gun, just went room to room like a ghost, popping them.”

“Shit.”

“Yeah, and yeah I’m scared, and you should be too.”

Earl didn’t say anything back, but ten G’s didn’t sound like a lot of money anymore.

~

As HE DROVE TOWARD VEGAS, TANNER GOT THE PHONE number for O'Grady's ranch from Cindy. After being jerked around by two of the man's flunkies, he was able to speak to Hank O'Grady.

"Who are you?" O'Grady said.

Tanner thought the voice sounded gruff and wondered if the man was in a bad mood. If he was, Tanner was about to make it worse.

"I'm the guy who killed your men in New Mexico."

"What?"

"You heard me."

"Why did you kill them?"

"You sent three goons with guns after two unarmed kids; that told me that you wanted the kids bad, so I figured they were worth something to you."

"You have them, Billy and Cindy?"

"I have them, and it'll cost you fifty grand to get them back."

"Listen punk, you tell me where you are and I'll send someone to get them, otherwise, I'll send men to get you, a lot of men."

"I'm not alone in this, O'Grady. I work for a man named Albert Rossetti in Vegas, and Albert Rossetti doesn't take shit from anyone."

"I don't know any Rossetti, and what's your name?"

Tanner searched his memory and came up with a name.

"My name is Ramone. Fifty grand, O'Grady, and we want it today. Send a man to Vegas with it and I'll call this afternoon and tell you where to meet. Okay, hayseed?"

When O'Grady replied, Tanner got exactly what he was hoping to hear—rage.

"I don't take orders from anybody, asshole! Do you

hear me? And I don't give a fuck who this Rossetti is. Goddamn Italians think they're hot shit, but I don't scare."

"Just get the money ready, pal, and then you'll get the kids back. It's just business."

O'Grady began speaking again but Tanner ended the call. When he looked over at Billy and Cindy, he saw worried faces.

"Tanner, are you really gonna sell us to O'Grady?" Cindy asked.

"No, that was me starting a war between him and Rossetti. If I can get them fighting each other, It'll distract them and make it easier for me to kill Rossetti, and for you to get away."

"That's smart," Cindy said, then she leaned over and kissed him on the cheek.

Tanner glanced at her, and again, he felt desire rise.

Billy leaned forward and caught his eye. "What if Mr. O'Grady sends men after you? And I mean a lot of men."

"They'll die," Tanner said, and his voice was so cold, so matter of fact, that it made Cindy reach over and take Billy's hand.

11

IT'S PERSONAL

SARA HAD HEARD BACK FROM THE FBI AGENT IN Colorado and learned that William Benton, age twenty, and Cindy Preston, age 19, were wanted for questioning by local authorities concerning an assault on the son of Colorado rancher, Hank O'Grady.

O'Grady claimed to have no idea why the three men that worked for him had been after Billy and Cindy, but he guessed that it was a misguided sense of loyalty that sent them in pursuit of the kids. When asked why the assault wasn't reported earlier, O'Grady said he hadn't wanted to get them in trouble.

Sara wasn't buying any of it, especially after learning that O'Grady was suspected of being involved in illegal businesses, and that he laundered their profits through his legal enterprises.

Garner finished reading the report and rested his feet atop the desk that Sara sat behind. They were still in the Las Vegas field office of the FBI, waiting for news.

"This O'Grady sent men after these kids, Billy and

Cindy, and Tanner must have thought they were coming for him, if it was Tanner," Garner said.

"It was Tanner, and yeah, that's my thinking too," Sara said.

The young agent, the one named Whitman walked over to speak with them. The word was out that Tanner was drawing closer and that Rossetti's men were going to intercept him before too long. Sara thanked Whitman for keeping them informed, then she asked for Rossetti's address.

"Why do you want to speak with Rossetti?" Garner said.

"I'm going to try to convince him to hand Tanner over to us if his men get the chance to take him alive. It'll not only cut down on the bloodshed, but we'll be able to question Tanner as well."

"I got the impression you wouldn't mind seeing Tanner dead?"

"I'd prefer it personally, but I also realize that Tanner could help bring others to justice."

Garner smiled. "You're a good agent, Sara, but you do know that Rossetti doesn't care what we want."

"Oh, I know that, but this will also give us a chance to see inside Rossetti's place. If I know Tanner, he'll make it past Rossetti's death squad and come after the man in his home. This way, we'll have an idea of the battleground before the shit hits the fan."

Garner grabbed his jacket, Sara gathered her purse, and they headed for the elevator.

As they were riding down, Garner stared at her.

"Do you know Tanner? Is that why it's personal for you?"

"He killed one of my confidential informants, my CI, a man named Brian Ames."

"I'm sorry."

"Don't be; just help me make the bastard pay."

"You got it."

As they drove toward Rossetti's, Sara glanced at Garner from the corner of her eye, wondering if he believed her about wanting to capture Tanner alive if possible.

She didn't give a damn about Tanner's safety, or about his worth as a source of information. She just wanted him to stay alive long enough for her to get to him, so that she could fire a bullet into his murderous heart.

Sara hated Tanner and had vowed to herself that she would be the one to kill him.

She sighed, sat back in her seat, and took in the sights of Las Vegas Boulevard, as Garner drove them toward Tanner's latest target, Albert Rossetti.

12

MEANWHILE, BACK AT THE RANCH

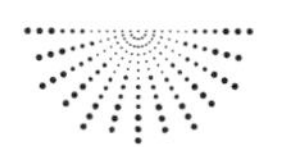

In Colorado, Hank O'Grady handed a glass of bourbon to Cindy's father, Joe Preston.

Preston accepted the drink with a tight smile.

"It's early to be drinking, isn't it Hank?"

O'Grady smirked. "Trust me. You're going to need that drink."

Preston took a sip of the excellent bourbon and awaited O'Grady's words with trepidation. He watched as O'Grady poured himself a drink and settled near him, by resting a hip on the corner of his massive oak desk. Behind the desk was a picture window that granted a view of a wide green field, and beyond that, the edge of the snowcapped Rocky Mountains.

Preston loved that view, had always loved it and envied O'Grady for having ownership of it. He'd grown up on the ranch just as O'Grady had, but his father had just been one of the ranch hands, while O'Grady's father had been Jacob O'Grady, lord and master of the Triple-E Ranch.

Hank O'Grady was a hard case, but his father, Jacob, had been a coldhearted bastard. Joe's father had hated

Jacob O'Grady, but he worked for the man all his life and called him sir. Now Joe was working for the son. However, Joe was ranch foreman, a respectable position, and was doing work that he loved.

When he realized O'Grady's son, Ricky, was in love with Cindy, he thought that good fortune had kissed him at last.

If Cindy married Ricky O'Grady, then he would no longer be just an employee, but family. Someday, it would be his grandson that ruled the Triple-E, and he would spend his later years inside the ranch house with servants, instead of being shuffled off to some old age home. But Cindy didn't like Ricky and had never liked Ricky.

Still, the boy was determined to marry her someday. Preston was certain that Ricky would have worn Cindy's resistance down in time, but then that damned Billy came along and stole her heart.

Preston hated Billy. If not for that son of a bitch he could have talked Cindy into accepting Ricky, he was sure he could have, but now they've run off to God knows where and Preston's job, his very way of life, was hanging by a thread.

Hank O'Grady raised his cut crystal glass up to catch the light from the window and studied the rainbow of colors.

"I sent the Cooper brothers to fetch Cindy and bring her back."

"Did they find her?" Preston asked.

"Oh yeah. Cindy and Billy were staying at some fleabag motel in New Mexico, but when the Cooper brothers went to grab Cindy, someone shot them dead."

Preston had taken his second sip of bourbon as O'Grady spoke. The liquid warmed him as the first sip had, but this time it felt like he had swallowed acid.

"They're dead? All three of them? Shit, was it that kid Billy that killed them?"

O'Grady laughed. "Billy Benton couldn't have killed any one of those men, much less all three of them. No, it was someone else, some asshole named Ramone. This Ramone says he works for a man named Rossetti. Rossetti is a Las Vegas mobster and he wants fifty thousand for Billy and Cindy."

Preston was trying to absorb the news when something occurred to him.

"How did the Cooper brothers track down Cindy and Billy?"

O'Grady's lips formed into a cruel but knowing smile. He was about fifty, a few years older than Preston, but he had a softness to his middle the lean, hardworking Preston would never have.

"I've got a way to track them down and I want you to go and bring them back."

"You're going to pay the money?"

"You'll hand over the money, get the kids, and then my boys will teach this Rossetti a lesson and take the money back."

"Then I won't be going alone?"

"Hell no, you'd just wind up dead too. No, I'll send a bunch of the boys with you and we'll get payback for the Coopers."

"I don't want Cindy hurt. I don't give a damn what happens to Billy, but I want Cindy back here safe and sound, so she can make things right with Ricky."

O'Grady stood up from the desk and hovered over Preston.

"If you want to make things right, you bring Cindy back here and have her marry Ricky. My boy wants her and no one else, and by God, he's going to have her. If you come back here without her, I'll kick your ass off the ranch."

Preston placed his glass atop the desk as he nodded in understanding.

"I'll bring her back and she'll do as she's told. I can get her to listen once Billy is out of the picture, I know I can."

O'Grady walked behind his desk and settled into a leather office chair. Preston took that as a dismissal and headed for the door. When he reached it, O'Grady spoke again.

"There's one more thing, Joe."

Preston swallowed hard, as he felt his palms grow slick with sweat. "Yes sir?"

"I want you to kill Billy Benton. I want that punk dead for hurting my boy."

"Hank, ah, I've never killed anything but an animal. I'm not sure I can do it."

"This is me you're talking to, Joe. Do you think I bought that bullshit about your wife running off with that short-order cook?"

Preston opened his mouth to respond, then closed it and stared down at the carpet.

"You killed your cheating whore of a wife, didn't you?" O'Grady asked.

"Lydia… Lydia ran away," Preston said, in words barely louder than a whisper.

He had killed his wife, had taken her up into the mountains, stabbed her to death, and buried her in a shallow grave.

"You'll kill Billy too, then I'll know you can be trusted. It'll also show Cindy that we're not fucking around. I mean hell, there are girls that would love to marry Ricky. He's rich, he's handsome, why is she being such a bitch about it?"

Preston shrugged. "She said she didn't love him."

O'Grady leaned back in his seat and made a sound of derision.

"Young girls are so stupid, but she'll learn, by God that girl will learn."

Preston left the office and walked to his quarters, a four-room cabin near the main bunkhouse.

He no sooner closed the door than he had to rush to the toilet and vomit.

He would kill Billy and might even enjoy it, but he knew that Cindy would then hate him. He could live with that too if he had to, after all, her mother had grown to hate him, and he lived with her for years before killing her. He could live with anything if it meant he stayed on the ranch. It was the only home he had ever known.

13
PARTNERS

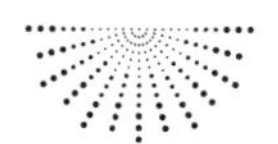

RAMONE EYED SARA WITH LUSTFUL INTEREST, AS HE escorted her and Garner into Rossetti's home.

Rossetti's place was an old ranch house that predated the casinos, but which had been modernized over the years. It was one level, but sprawling and L-shaped. The top of the L was at the rear of the home, while a large pool separated it from what used to be a bunkhouse for the ranch hands. The bunkhouse was currently used as an occasional barracks for Rossetti's goons.

The front of the property faced a county road, while the rest of it was surrounded by hills on three sides, beyond which laid scrubland.

To reach the home, you had to cruise down a winding driveway, and there were places to park in front and on the right side.

A woman stepped out of a hallway on the left and informed Ramone that Rossetti wanted to speak to him. The woman was young, with red hair, and wore a short skirt. She was one of Rossetti's call girls.

She would be switched for another of her ilk and put

back to work on The Vegas Strip whenever the fat man grew tired of banging her.

Ramone asked the two FBI agents to stay where they were, then told the woman, whom he called Joy, to stay and watch them. Ramone had barely left the foyer when Garner elicited a smile from Joy. Within seconds, the redhead was laughing and touching him, her fingers walking along his chest, as they whispered to each other.

Sara shook her head in irritation as she watched them and wondered if Garner ever thought with anything other than his dick. They had come there to scout the place and feel out Rossetti, not to try to hook up with one of the man's high-priced whores.

Garner and Joy separated as the sound of footsteps approached, and Ramone reappeared with Rossetti. Sara had seen pictures of the man and expected him to be fat, but the photos didn't do his girth justice. She looked at Joy, as the whore turned to leave, and hoped that Rossetti was paying her a fortune to sleep with him. She had earned it.

Once the four of them were alone, Rossetti looked Sara over.

"You're right, Ramone, she's a hot piece of ass, but what I want to know, lady, is if you're here to hassle me or to help protect me?"

"Protect you from what?"

"Don't play games, you know that a man named Tanner is gunning for me or you wouldn't be here."

"I also know that Tanner never fails to carry out a hit. So, if you want protection, we'll give it to you."

Rossetti squinted. "What's the catch?"

"Come back to the office and spill your guts about everything you know, and we'll place you in Witness Protection. I guarantee that Tanner will never find you once we make you disappear."

Rossetti laughed. "Turn snitch on my friends? Fuck that, I'll handle Tanner my way."

Sara moved closer to Rossetti. "How's it feel to only have hours left to live?"

"Tanner is the one about to become extinct. He'll never make it here. Even if he did, Ramone could handle him."

Sara looked Ramone over and thought that he looked capable, but she knew Tanner, in that, she had studied the man and was aware he was a killing machine. Sara was certain that Ramone would die if he faced off with Tanner.

Sara smiled, as she tried another approach. "Why don't you invite me and my partner into your office for a drink, Mr. Rossetti? Perhaps we can work something out?"

Ramone's phone rang before Rossetti could answer her. Ramone spoke to someone and then listened, followed by a smile. When he put his phone away, he whispered something to Rossetti.

Rossetti's grin looked more like a grimace in his jowly face. "I think my problem is about to be solved."

"You know where Tanner is? Tell us his location and I'll chopper there and arrest him."

"Arrest him? Lady, when my boys get done with him it'll be like he never existed. Now, get the hell out of my house."

SARA SLAMMED THE PASSENGER DOOR AS THEY GOT BACK IN the car.

Tanner was out there somewhere, and Rossetti knew where. The man also seemed confident that his men would kill Tanner. Sara wondered how many thugs Tanner was going up against. When she glanced at Garner, she gave him a look of disgust.

"You were certainly useless in there."

Garner appeared taken aback by her anger but then shrugged.

"You should be happy; I got what we came for."

"What are you talking about?"

"The girl, Joy, she told me the layout of the house."

"When?"

Garner reached over and took Sara's hand. She resisted at first, but then relented and he extended her index finger and began moving its tip along his chest, as he traced the layout of Rossetti's home, just as Joy had done.

"Past the living room, there are five rooms off the hallway. One is a bathroom and the other four are bedrooms. The hallway leads to the kitchen, where another hallway branches off to two more bedrooms, the last of which is Rossetti's, and he keeps his office at the back of the home, facing a pool."

Sara took her hand back and stared at Garner. "Why did Joy tell you all that? Do you know her?"

"I've never met her before."

"Then why would she help you?"

Garner stared into her eyes, holding her gaze. "She wanted to please me, Sara; women love to please me."

Sara gazed at him a little longer, then broke eye contact. She didn't speak until they had left the secluded home and were back on the highway.

"Not all women want to please you."

"Right," Garner said.

"I find you completely resistible."

"Uh-huh."

"Thanks for getting that info; it may come in handy."

"You're welcome, partner."

Partners, Sara thought, *that's all we'll ever be to each other, partners.*

Still, it bothered her that she had felt a thrill when Garner took her hand, and that her fingers tingled from his touch.

She pushed Garner from her mind and thought about Tanner, about Rossetti's goons closing in on him. Sara wondered if Tanner would survive long enough for her to kill him.

14
TRAPPED!

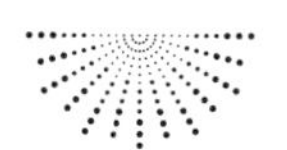

Tanner spotted the car following him in Arizona, but when he saw that there was just one guy in the vehicle, he began to question whether he was imagining it.

As he crossed into Nevada, the car fell back, and Tanner relaxed. That didn't last for long, because before a minute passed, a silver Land Rover with four guys in it rode up on his tail. When Tanner spotted the barrel of a shotgun sticking up, he knew shit was about to go down.

Aldo told his man to move closer to Tanner's pickup, then he spotted Tanner's intense eyes in the rearview mirror.

"All right, that did it. He knows we're here."

The driver spoke. "Who are the other two? They look like kids."

"Tanner must have been using them for cover. Once we run them to ground, you stay with the kids while we kill Tanner, but don't kill them. I want to talk to them first."

"He's speeding up!"

"Stay with him," Aldo said. "It's time for Tanner to die."

Merle and Earl were having a hard time keeping up, but they could tell that Aldo and his men were tracking a white pickup truck.

"Get closer," Merle said.

"I'm tryin', but we ain't got the right engine for this, and them dudes are flyin'."

"Just stay ready and hope we get a break. With a little luck, we'll get Tanner."

"A little luck?"

"All right, a lot of luck, but just stay close and don't lose them."

"Merle?"

"Yeah?"

"I don't want to die, so I say we just stay back and watch what happens."

Merle agreed and then gripped his weapon tighter.

Tanner cut across a lane and exited the highway so quickly that Aldo's man was unable to keep up and missed the exit.

Aldo's driver told everyone to hold on and he took the Land Rover across desert landscape at high speed, while bumping over brush and sand dunes.

Tanner had placed a gap between them, but he was still in sight and headed down a road where ranch land stretched out to either side, with homes spaced far apart.

The pickup had a good engine, but the Land Rover was better, and before they traveled a mile, the gap had shrunk.

When Tanner made a skidding right turn into the driveway of a home surrounded by land, Aldo tapped a fist on the dashboard.

"We got the fucker!"

~

CINDY LET OUT A SCREAM AS TANNER MADE THE TURN, then grunted when the pickup came to a hard stop near the front porch of the home.

Before either she or Billy could respond to what had happened, Tanner was out of the truck and moving up the stairs. He ran into the front door without slowing and slammed it with a shoulder.

The door banged open, Tanner went inside and moments later Aldo and his men slid to a stop at the entrance to the driveway, then ran toward the pickup.

Aldo's driver pointed his weapon at Billy and Cindy and told them to get out of the truck. The two kids did as ordered while raising their hands above their heads.

"Stay with them, Benny," Aldo told the driver, before clapping a hand on the shoulder of another man. "Craig, you take the back."

The man, Craig, ran low along the side of the home. After pausing at the rear corner, he disappeared around the back of the house, which was two stories high and well cared for.

Their vehicles were the only ones on the property, and Aldo hoped that meant the owners were out, or at work. He didn't need a simple killing to turn into a bloodbath.

Aldo took one measuring glance at Billy and Cindy,

then headed for the home with the fourth man flanking him on the left. Aldo carried an old Mossberg 500 shotgun, while the man with him sported a new Glock.

The home's front door hung in a frame that was splintered where the lock had torn free and the door was sitting halfway open.

Aldo craned his neck as he reached the stairs and could see what looked like a living room. A noise came from inside the home. It sounded like someone banging on sheet metal or something, but just as Aldo cocked his head to hear it better, the noise ended, and the house fell silent.

Aldo and his man climbed up the stairs with caution and soon they were standing atop the porch where, through the half-open door, they could make out more of the living room and glimpse the dining room table beyond it.

The house looked well-lit, as the blinds had been left open and the day was bright, but Aldo saw no moving shadows that would give Tanner's position away.

More sound came from inside the home, a clattering noise, but the sound was indistinct and brief.

Aldo took out his phone and dialed Craig, the man he had sent to cover the rear.

"You see anything?"

"No, boss, and the back door is locked, but did you hear that banging?"

"Yeah, I heard it, but I don't know what it means."

"Do you want me to kick the back door in?"

"Yeah, but wait until after I ring you again to do it."

"Got it," Craig said, and then they both hung up.

Aldo slipped the phone into his pocket, nodded toward the man at his side, and let his shotgun lead the way into the house.

Tanner was trapped.

15

ROOM NUMBER FOUR

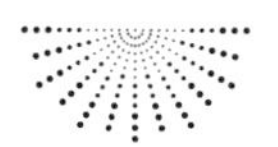

In Spring Valley, Lillian wiped at tears as Dwight loaded luggage into her car.

She turned and kissed her husband.

"Come with me. Tanner is just one man. Even if Rossetti doesn't stop him, we can still hide from him."

Dwight caressed her cheek. "I told you before that I won't put you at risk, and I meant that. Go to your mother's house, be safe and… I'll stay here and wait for Tanner."

"We can hire bodyguards. Six men, more even."

"It won't do any good. Tanner would cut through them and still kill me, but I'm hoping he'll give me a chance to talk if I'm alone."

"Talk? What good will that do?"

"I don't know, maybe nothing, but I have information Tanner can use to get in and out of Rossetti's home safely. Maybe I can trade it for my life."

Lillian wrapped her arms around Dwight for a long while before releasing him with a kiss.

"I'll call you," she said.

"All right, but only once each night and… if I don't answer…"

"Don't think about that. Tanner will take the trade, but can he be trusted?"

Dwight thought about that, and a thin smile formed on his face. "You know, in an odd way, Tanner is an honorable man. He'll do what he says he'll do."

They said their words of goodbye and Lillian drove away while watching Dwight's form dwindle in her rearview mirror, as she neared the four-lane road at the end of their block.

LILLIAN NEVER LEFT THE AREA.

She took room Number Four at the motel that sat across the road from the entrance to her block. As she'd hoped, the view from the window gave her the sight line she needed to see her front door and the right side of her home.

Satisfied with her field of vision, Lillian unpacked one of her bags and took out the Beretta 92 that had belonged to her father. She had never fired the weapon, or any other weapon, but the gun was loaded and she was ready to use it to save her husband's life.

She settled herself in front of the motel window with binoculars and began watching her house.

When Tanner showed, she'd run across the road and slip back inside the house through the window she'd left unlocked in the dining room. If Tanner wanted Dwight's life, then he would have to go through her to get it. Lillian was certain the element of surprise would work in her favor.

And unfortunately for Tanner, the lady was right.

16
IT'S ALWAYS THE LAST PLACE YOU LOOK

ALDO STOOD IN THE QUIET HOUSE HOLDING A SHOTGUN AS he stared down the hallway that led to the kitchen. Without taking his eyes from the hall, he whispered to the man at his side.

"Ronny, check out the upstairs, but be damn careful when you raise your head above the level of the landing. The son of a bitch could be lying beneath a bed just waiting for something to shoot at."

"Got ya," Ronny said, then the thin man drifted up the stairs slow and easy, while making no more sound than a cat.

Aldo left the living room and stepped through the dining area, where there was a short alcove near the back that had a marble counter with green shutters above it.

The counter was likely used to pass food from the kitchen into the dining room. Aldo took the time to stack several dining room chairs into the alcove and was confident that Tanner would be heard if he tried to leave the kitchen that way.

A floorboard creaked above his head and told him that

Ronny was conducting his search. Aldo moved into the hallway, where he came across the first door. It was on his left, and after standing to the right of it, he turned the knob and pushed it inward.

Nothing happened.

When he peeked around the corner, he saw what looked like a guest bedroom. After searching beneath the bed and checking out the room's tiny closet, Aldo moved on and found an open doorway on the other side of the hall, which turned out to be a bathroom.

He winced while looking at the toilet. He'd been headed to take a leak when the call came in that Tanner was spotted, and now his bladder wanted to burst.

It'll have to wait, Aldo thought, then he smiled as he imagined relieving himself on Tanner's corpse.

There was no one in the shower stall, so Aldo moved on. The last doorway opened onto a home office that had dozens of family pictures on the walls. Several of the women in the photos were blondes and it reminded him of Cindy.

Why the hell is Tanner traveling around with those kids?

Aldo shrugged at his own question. He could find out the answer to that once he killed Tanner.

No one was hiding behind the desk or in the office closet. As he walked back into the hallway, he studied the door set in the opposite wall, and saw that there was a metal slide bolt locking it from the outside.

It was the basement door and Aldo dismissed it. There was no way Tanner could have slid that bolt in place from the other side.

Aldo could see part of the kitchen from where he stood, and in a corner of it was the back door, still shut.

He took out his phone to call his man, Craig, at the rear of the house, just as Ronny returned from upstairs.

"There's no one up there," Ronny whispered. "He's got to be in the kitchen, right?"

Aldo nodded and made his call, let it ring once, and waited for Craig to kick the back door in. He didn't have to wait long. After the sound of breaking wood, he rushed into the kitchen with the Mossberg at the ready and found… nothing.

"What the hell?" Ronny said.

Aldo swiveled his head around in a wild jerky motion, as he looked for a place big enough to conceal a man.

When his eyes fell upon the doors beneath the double sink, he sent a blast from the shotgun their way and shredded them, then pumped the shotgun and fired again and again.

When he was through, Craig reached over and ripped one of the ruined doors open, revealing an assortment of leaking containers that held cleaning products. There was also a garbage pail with more holes than a cheese grater.

Aldo lowered the shotgun and stared at his men.

"Where the fuck did he—"

Aldo never finished the sentence. Rather, his speech morphed into a scream, as metal pellets bombarded him and Ronny, causing both men to fall atop the linoleum floor in agony.

And yet, even through the pain, Aldo marveled at what he was seeing, as Tanner stuck his head out of the oven and fired his next shot at Craig, ripping holes in the man's throat and killing him.

After banging through the front door, Tanner had two plans for survival.

The first plan was to use anyone in the home as a

diversion for a rear attack, but once he realized the house was empty, he went to his second plan, which was to take cover and launch a surprise attack.

He went through all the rooms on the first floor as Aldo would later do, but his pace had been quicker, more frantic and with an eye solely toward seeking a place of concealment.

After checking out the kitchen, he returned to the locked basement door and slid the bolt aside to flick on the switch, illuminating a set of wooden stairs, and walls made from unfinished wallboard.

That's when he heard voices out front shouting at Billy and Cindy and knew his time was growing short.

Tanner estimated the distance in his head, went down six steps and used the butt of his shotgun to batter through the wallboard that sat flush behind the stove. The gypsum broke apart easily under the assault and Tanner widened the hole and kept going, ramming the shotgun against the metal backing of the old oven he'd seen, causing it to bend inward at the middle and gap outward at its sides.

With that done, he placed the shotgun atop a step. With both hands, he wrenched the back of the oven free at its top and took it through the hole in the wallboard, bending it downwards between two wall studs, where it laid suspended above the stairs like a shelf.

Then, he listened for movement. After hearing only silence he went back up the basement stairs, where he closed and locked the door before entering the kitchen, opening the oven door, and climbing into it backwards, sending the oven racks through the hole to clatter down the basement steps.

As he reached out to close the oven door, he heard footfalls toward the front of the house and settled inside his place of concealment to wait.

He had to keep his legs straight and still, otherwise the metal backing from the oven would rattle and make noise. Tanner knew that anyone opening the basement door would see his lower half suspended above the steps and tear his legs to pieces with gunfire.

Tanner listened for any sound, even as his eyes searched for movement through the smeared, thick glass rectangle set in the oven door. The cramped space was hot and stank of grease and burnt meat. While grimacing, Tanner realized that when he fired the shotgun in the tight space the sound would be deafening.

He waited like that, as his legs cramped from strain and sweat ran down his face and into his eyes.

When the wait ended, it was abrupt. First, Aldo's shadow appeared, then the back door was kicked in. Afterward, Aldo and Ronny joined Craig in the middle of the room.

The first blast from Aldo's Mossberg made Tanner grit his teeth, and after Craig ripped open the door beneath the sink, Tanner knew it was time to act.

He was right about the sound, as the blast from his own gun deafened him and set his ears to ringing, but he followed it up with another shot as he shoved open the oven and blasted Craig.

TANNER CRAWLED OUT OF THE OVEN, HIS HEAD SWIVELING about for signs of movement, as the ringing in his ears blocked out all other sound.

The man who had kicked open the back door was dead, but one of the other men was reaching for a Glock. Tanner beat him to it and used the gun to place two bullets into his head.

He wanted to ask the remaining man where the fourth man was, but he knew he would never hear the answer over the ringing sound in his ears. He suspected that the fourth man had been left outside to guard Billy and Cindy.

Tanner tossed his empty shotgun away and grabbed up Aldo's superior Mossberg. With practiced efficiency, he pumped another shell into the chamber and placed the gun against Aldo's chest.

~

ALDO FOUND IT HARD TO FOCUS ON ANYTHING OTHER THAN the agony in his shredded legs, and he moaned in disgust as he watched Tanner blow Ronny's brains out.

When he saw that Tanner meant to kill him with his own gun, he cursed, and then he asked Tanner a question.

"How the hell did you fit inside that oven?"

There was no answer. Tanner just stared down at him with a set of cold eyes, and for Aldo, the world ended.

~

OUTSIDE THE HOUSE ALDO'S MAN, BENNY, WAS SMILING after hearing the familiar blasts of Aldo's Mossberg.

Benny was the youngest and newest member of Aldo's crew. He was a muscular man with prison tats on his neck and a single braid hanging down his back.

Benny grinned at Billy and Cindy, who were sitting on the ground while propped against the side of the pickup.

"Your asshole friend Tanner is dead, and if I had to guess, Aldo will want to plant you too."

Cindy responded to his words by crying, while Billy tensed up, as if he was about to leap to his feet.

Benny pointed his gun at him. "Try it. Try it and I'll

blow your head off."

Billy settled back against the pickup and Cindy reached over and took his hand.

A minute passed, then two, and then nearly five, and Benny's eyebrows knitted together.

He wanted to call Aldo to find out what was happening, but just in case things hadn't ended inside, he didn't want to distract his boss or give away his position by causing Aldo's phone to ring or vibrate.

Benny reached down and grabbed a fistful of Cindy's hair, causing her to rise to her feet, while keeping his gun leveled at Billy.

"Stay seated, kid, me and the sweet piece are just going to take a look inside the house. If you try to run, I'll kill her."

Billy put up a hand. "I won't move, just please don't hurt her."

"Stay seated and she'll be fine. Now c'mon, Blondie, let's see what's going on in there."

Benny guided Cindy along by the grip he still held on her hair, and as they stepped toward the house, something caught his eye. A car was coming. Benny turned back toward the road and watched as an old Chevy pulled to the curb and parked. Benny studied the car and thought the driver was alone.

The kid by the pickup twitched and Benny pointed his gun at him, but the kid wasn't looking at him. He was staring at something behind Benny, and the kid was smiling.

Benny jerked his head around, saw Tanner rushing toward him, then felt the carving knife enter his chest. Benny released Cindy and sank to his knees.

As a chill passed through Benny, he actually felt his heart stop beating, and knew he was dead.

17
JUST WHEN YOU THINK YOU'VE GOT IT MADE

After Tanner killed Benny, the Chevy that had been parked out on the road jumped the curb while making a harsh scraping sound, it then headed across the uneven ground of the lawn.

Tanner swung the Mossberg up to blast it, but Billy was blocking his shot as he ran over toward Cindy. Tanner cursed and then, not being a fool, he swiveled his head about looking for other attackers. That's when he spotted Earl sprinting toward him from a corner of the house.

When he spun in that direction, Cindy was blocking his shot. Before Tanner could adjust, Earl plowed into her and shoved Cindy into Tanner, causing him to lose his balance just as the car driven by Merle clipped Billy and knocked him down.

Tanner recovered, rolled and was bringing the shotgun up when he saw Cindy frantically gesturing behind him. Tanner dived out of the way just in time to avoid being run over by Merle.

He hadn't been aware the car had changed direction

because his ears still rang from the shot he had fired inside the oven.

Earl tried to wrest the shotgun away, even as Merle exited the car. Tanner kicked Earl in the chest, forcing him away, but Merle reached out with a stun gun and blasted Tanner, causing him to drop his weapon and collapse atop the grass.

Billy came limping over just as they loaded Tanner into the back seat of the Chevy, but Earl swung the Mossberg around and Billy froze in his tracks.

The Chevy stuttered as if it were about to cut off, but it kept running, and Merle headed the car down the lawn and back toward the road.

The vehicle gave off white smoke as it hemorrhaged engine coolant, and when Merle drove it off the curb, the muffler ripped loose.

~

Merle felt like his heart was doing a thousand beats a second. He kept checking the back seat, where Earl was holding the shotgun on Tanner.

When the muffler came off the Chevy, Merle stopped the car in the middle of the street and the engine died.

"This car is done. We'll take Aldo's Land Rover."

Earl looked horrified by the suggestion. "Are you crazy?"

"Aldo's probably dead. I'm pretty sure he won't mind."

Tanner was still affected by the first blast when Merle gave him a second taste of the stun gun, then he was carried to the Land Rover.

Merle pointed back at Billy and Cindy. "Go make sure those two don't follow us."

Earl took out a knife and ran back toward the young couple.

Billy pushed Cindy behind him and put up his hands to fight, but Earl stopped short of them and plunged the blade into a rear tire of the pickup, causing a flat.

Then the Carter brothers took off, leaving Cindy and Billy to look on with sad eyes, as they worried over Tanner's fate.

18
THAT SMILE

MERLE HANDED HIS BROTHER A LARGE PLASTIC ZIP TIE AND Earl bound Tanner's wrists together.

Merle gazed at Tanner in the rearview mirror and it thrilled him to see the man dazed and helpless.

"We got him! Damn it if we don't got him!"

Earl patted him on the shoulder. He was so giddy that he was giggling, but when he looked over at Tanner and met the man's eyes, the giggle died in his throat.

"Who are you two? Do you work for Rossetti?" Tanner asked, and was glad he could hear his own voice, and that the ringing in his ears had faded away.

"We work for ourselves and we're gonna get a shitload of money for you."

"How much?"

"Ten grand."

"Dead or alive?"

Earl shrugged. "Either one."

"Rossetti will pay more for me alive, especially when he finds out I killed four of his men back there. You can probably get twenty."

Earl caught his brother's eye in the mirror.

"He's right. He's worth more alive than dead, because that way Rossetti can kill him himself."

Merle stared at Tanner. "He's just sayin' that so we won't kill him, still… after whackin' Aldo and his boys, yeah, Rossetti will probably pay more."

There was a cell phone sitting in the cup holder. Its shrill ring made the brothers jump in their seats.

"Rossetti's calling," Tanner said.

Merle reached for the phone as if it was too hot to touch, but after six rings, he answered it.

"Hello?"

"Benny?"

"Um, my name is Merle Carter, is this Rossetti?"

"This is Ramone, why are you answering Benny's phone?"

"It was in the Land Rover."

"Where the hell is Aldo?"

"Aldo's dead. Tanner killed him and his whole crew."

The line went silent and Merle rode on with the phone pressed against his ear, as he drove along US-93.

"Listen, Merle, or whoever you are, do you have any idea where Tanner might be now?"

"We got him! My brother and me, we got Tanner and we took him alive. He's right here in Aldo's ride."

More silence as Ramone processed the news. Seconds later, Merle could hear him speak to someone else, but couldn't make out what was being said. Then a new voice came on the line.

"This is Albert Rossetti, if you've got Tanner, put him on the phone."

"Ah, yeah, um sure thing, Mr. Rossetti, hold on a second."

Merle passed the phone over his shoulder, as he spoke to his brother.

"It's Rossetti himself and he wants to speak with Tanner."

Earl took the phone clumsily with his left hand and then held it up next to Tanner's right ear.

"Hello? Tanner?"

"Hello, Rossetti."

"Listen, how do I know it's you?"

"It's me. I was hired to kill you and that's just what I'm going to do."

"Hey, tough guy, I don't think you're gonna do shit. You know what's funny? The guy that hired you, we're best buds now and I'm under the Conglomerate's protection, so everything you've done is for nothing."

"I was hired to do a job and I'm going to do it. Nothing changes that, Rossetti, nothing."

"We'll see, punk, now put that Merle guy back on."

Tanner jerked his head away from the phone and Earl handed the cell phone back to his brother, who received instructions on where to meet up with Ramone.

Merle slipped the phone back in the cup holder and spoke to Earl.

"We're taking him to a house on Stewart Avenue in Vegas. A dude named Ramone will meet us there."

Tanner gazed out at the desert landscape, content to let himself be ferried to Vegas by the Carter brothers. After all, that's where his target was, and Rossetti would be that much easier to kill if he thought he had nothing to fear.

"Merle?"

Merle looked at his brother via the mirror. "What?"

"Tanner's smilin'. Why's he smilin'?"

"Just keep that shotgun on him."

"All right, but I don't like that smile."

Merle moved his head until he could see Tanner in the mirror, and no, he didn't like that smile either.

19

HE MUST BE DEAD

Sara and Garner jumped from a helicopter, then squinted as protection against the sand billowing about in the wake from the chopper's blades.

The house was several hundred feet away, but Sara spotted the body on the front lawn as soon as she looked in that direction. He had been a muscular man with a long braid, and there was a knife sticking out of his chest.

Garner pointed at the body as they drew closer. "Looks like he got it in the heart. There's not much blood."

Sara nodded in agreement, then noticed the local PD approaching. The cop was a forty-something woman with short dark hair and blue-green eyes. She ignored Garner but looked Sara over with much interest.

"I'm Detective Gladstone. I understand that you know who caused all this chaos?"

"Yes," Sara said. "We believe it was a man named Tanner, but I understand you have a witness?"

Gladstone pointed at a hill across the road. "Mr. Howard, his house is on the other side of that hill, but he didn't witness any violence."

"What did he see?" Sara asked.

"He saw two men carry another man into an SUV from that car abandoned in the street there. He also saw a young male and a young female, both Caucasian, standing near our first corpse, the man on the lawn there."

"Do you have the man and woman in custody?"

"Mr. Howard said the boy changed a tire on a pickup and hauled ass away from here. And he said it had Arizona plates, so they might be headed out of state."

Garner spoke up. "We'd like to look in the house when we can."

"Sure, and I understand you have a forensic team on the way as well, correct?"

Garner smiled. "Yes, and we appreciate your help."

Gladstone smiled back at him. "Always happy to help."

After Gladstone left, Garner looked at Sara and saw worried eyes above a frown.

"What's wrong?"

"She said that the witness saw a man being carried away. It sounds like Tanner's luck may have finally run out."

Sara's phone vibrated, and she answered it. It was Agent Whitman. Sara placed the call on speakerphone.

"Go ahead, Agent Whitman, what's this news you have?"

"It's Rossetti. He and another man left his home together, but our agents lost them after they entered a casino."

"Anything else?"

"Yes, the four bodies on the scene there were all employees of Rossetti. All four men are listed as private security."

"Private army is more like it. Thank you, Whitman, and stay in touch."

Garner grimaced. "It took six men, but it sounds like Tanner's finished. If Rossetti hasn't killed him yet, he soon will."

Sara felt a strange mixture of emotions. She wanted Tanner dead, but only by her hand. It was also likely that his body would never turn up, but rather be buried forever out in the desert.

That's when Sara wished for something that she never thought she would, she wished for Tanner's continued survival.

She turned and headed into the house to look at more of Tanner's handiwork.

20

AND HE CAN FIGHT TOO

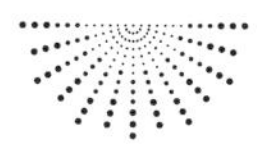

Merle was thinking of ways to spend his share of the money when the Land Rover was struck from the side and forced into oncoming traffic.

"Shit!"

Merle saw a tractor-trailer headed straight for him with its air horn blaring, but before he could recover from his shock and move back into his lane, the Land Rover was struck again. This time the impact forced him off the roadway completely and into the scrubland past the shoulder.

Tanner was jounced about just as Merle and Earl were, but he used it to turn toward Earl and kicked out at the shotgun, knocking it out of Earl's hands and onto the floor, while a second kick caught Earl on the chin and stunned him.

Once Merle brought the vehicle to a shuddering stop, Tanner opened the door, stood with his bound hands raised high and then brought his arms down in a rush. The plastic zip tie struck the edge of the steel door and popped open, as its ratcheting teeth gave way to the immense pressure.

Merle saw that Tanner was free and grabbed the stun gun off the seat. That's when Billy shattered the driver's side window with a tire iron. Merle cried out as a thousand bits of glass covered him, and Tanner reached over the back seat and ripped the stun gun away, before plucking the shotgun from the floor.

Cindy ran to Tanner and grabbed his arm. "Are you okay?"

Tanner saw the concern in her eyes and smiled. "I'm good, thanks to you and your boyfriend."

Someone shouted, "Hey!" and Tanner saw that the driver of the truck they nearly hit had parked his rig and was charging toward them, his face scarlet from anger.

Tanner handed Billy the weapons and walked over to meet the man. The trucker was huge, well over six feet tall and wide with muscle.

The man stopped walking and glared at Tanner. "Were you the asshole driving that car?"

Tanner said nothing, quickened his pace, and slammed a fist into the trucker's gut.

A sound like, "Ooooouuummmffff," emerged from the trucker as he bent forward, and then Tanner slammed him on the side of the head with an elbow, causing the man to grunt and fall facedown into the sand.

With that done, Tanner returned to the Land Rover and stared in at the Carter brothers.

"Billy, Cindy, go wait in the pickup and I'll be right there."

Cindy nibbled her bottom lip, then spoke to Tanner. "Are you going to kill them?"

"That depends on them," Tanner said, and Cindy followed Billy back to the pickup.

Merle gazed at Tanner with hopeful eyes. "You ain't gonna kill us?"

"Not if you do what I say. And it should also save you from Rossetti too."

"Rossetti?" Earl said.

"I don't think he'll be happy that you let me get away, do you?"

The brothers looked at each other as their faces turned pale.

"What do you want us to do?" Merle asked.

THE TRUCKER WAS SITTING UP AND GIVING TANNER THE finger as they drove away in the battered pickup.

Cindy was full of nervous energy as she explained to Tanner that Billy had changed the flat and went racing after them.

"We were doing a hundred miles an hour and looking ahead for the Land Rover, praying that they hadn't gone in a different direction. Then Billy spotted it, went even faster and rammed them before they knew what happened."

Billy looked past Cindy at Tanner. "Did you kill the men who were after you in the house?"

"Yes."

"Why didn't you kill those two back there?"

"They're useful to me."

Tanner knew that they were heading away from Vegas after being spun around, but as he passed a road sign, he realized he could take care of other business that he had nearby and hung a right onto Route 215.

"Where are we going?" Cindy said.

"I have to pay a visit to a friend," Tanner said and

aimed the truck toward Dwight Sorrell's home in Spring Valley.

21
SHOULD I, OR SHOULDN'T I?

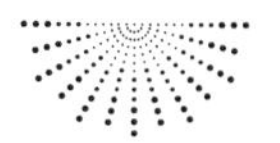

TANNER PARKED THE PICKUP TRUCK THREE HOUSES AWAY and called Sorrell.

The voice that answered was hesitant, but familiar.

"Hello? Tanner?"

"It's me, Dwight. Are you alone?"

"I'm alone and I'm at my house. I know better than to try to hide from you, but I do hope that you'll give me a chance to talk."

"We'll talk, but it won't change what you did."

"I know that."

Tanner ended the call and got out of the truck with Billy and Cindy.

"This is where we go our separate ways," Tanner said.

Cindy pouted and gave him a quick hug, while Billy shook his hand.

Tanner stared into Billy's eyes with his intense gaze. "You take care of Cindy."

Billy put an arm around her shoulders. "That's the plan."

Tanner had taken shells for the Mossberg from the

center console of the Land Rover. He carried the shotgun pointed downward, and kept it flush against his leg as he walked toward Dwight's house.

Billy gave the horn a toot as he and Cindy drove away, and Dwight opened his door before Tanner could ring the bell.

Dwight swallowed hard as he looked at the shotgun. "Come on in."

"If this is an ambush, if there's someone else in there, I'll kill all of you."

Dwight spread his hands. "There are no tricks, Tanner. I just want to talk."

Tanner entered with the shotgun up and ready, but he found no one lying in wait.

They went into Dwight's office and Tanner took the seat behind the desk, where he could keep an eye on the door. Dwight stood in front of the desk with his face looking pale and shadowy, despite the sunlight beaming through the window.

Tanner smirked at him. "So, what do you want to say to me?"

"I betrayed you and I was the one who planted the drugs on you, but I only did it because Rossetti threatened to kill Lillian."

Tanner squinted at him. "Why didn't you tell me about it?"

"I was afraid. I knew it wouldn't keep you from going after Rossetti and I didn't want Lillian caught in the crossfire."

"After you betrayed me, did Rossetti let her go?"

"Yes, she's fine, and I know it doesn't change what I did to you, but I wanted you to know that it wasn't about money or anything like that."

"Are you done?"

"No."

"What else?"

"I can help you get to Rossetti."

"How?"

"There's a tunnel that runs past the pool and leads from Rossetti's office to an exit behind the old bunkhouse. There's a shack there atop a hill, an old tool shed."

"How do you know that?"

Dwight shrugged. "I'm in real estate, commercial real estate, but I have a friend on the residential side who once handled the property. He told me about it. The tunnel was built the same time the original pool was put in, back in the sixties when some mobster owned the place… some other mobster."

"How do I get in and out?"

Dwight explained where the tunnel's entrance and exit were located and pointed to an envelope lying atop the desk.

"That envelope is for you. It was delivered by one of Frank Richards' men."

"The client? He must be mad that the hit has taken so long."

"No, he and Rossetti settled their dispute while you were… away. If anything, I think he wants to call it off."

"Is that how you found out I was free?"

"Yeah."

"Two guys tried to kill me in Brownsville. I thought Rossetti was behind that, but maybe it was Richards."

"It could have been both. Don't trust Richards."

Tanner stared at him. "Do you want to talk about trust, Dwight?"

Dwight opened his mouth, but then closed it, as he seemed to shrink beneath Tanner's gaze.

Tanner unsealed the envelope and saw that it

contained only a phone number. He memorized it, folded it once, then stuck it in his shirt pocket.

"I need a car. I'm taking yours."

"The keys are in the kitchen on a hook by the back door."

"Do you have anything else you want to say?"

Dwight wiped his brow. He had begun to sweat and was taking short, shallow breaths.

"No… that's all I had to say."

Tanner gripped the shotgun and stared at him, still deciding Dwight's fate.

"Why are you unarmed? You knew I was coming."

"I betrayed you. I did it to save Lillian, but I still did it."

Tanner stood and the movement so unnerved Dwight that his knees nearly gave out.

"I'm not going to kill you, Dwight, but we're through."

Dwight breathed a sigh of relief, then he leapt across the desk and began fighting Tanner for control of the shotgun.

22
IT WAS AN ACCIDENT...HONEST

LILLIAN'S EYES HAD BECOME BLEARY FROM SPENDING SO much time looking at her house through binoculars. She rubbed the bridge of her nose and realized that she had to use the bathroom.

When she returned to the window and raised the binoculars up, she nearly fell out of her seat. Dwight and Tanner were talking at her front door. Lillian felt her heart hammer away as she spotted the shotgun gripped in Tanner's hands.

She grabbed her purse, rushed from the motel room, and found a wall of traffic blocking her path. Lillian hopped about from foot to foot as if the ground was too hot to stand on, but then she caught a gap in the traffic and rushed across the road while removing the gun from her purse.

Once she reached the other side, she struggled to control her rising panic, and was so nervous that she dropped her purse. After going back for it, she dropped it again, picked it up by its bottom and sent her wallet and everything else tumbling out onto the ground. Lillian cursed the bag in spades and left it and its contents where they lay, as her only thought was to save her husband.

As she drew closer, she saw Tanner stand up from behind the desk with the shotgun pointing toward Dwight. Lillian took aim while running at the window and fired just as Dwight tackled Tanner to the floor.

Dwight's leap took Tanner by surprise and he was sure the man was trying to kill him.

Then Tanner registered the muffled shot, the falling glass, and realized that someone was firing from outside.

Dwight had his hands on the shotgun as he screamed in Tanner's face. "Don't shoot her! Don't shoot her!"

Tanner wedged a leg up between them and kicked Dwight away and up in front of the window.

Lillian fired again, not realizing it was her husband. The bullet ricocheted off the window frame and into the room.

"Lillian don't shoot! It's okay! Tanner won't hurt us."

Tanner stood and placed the barrel of the shotgun under Dwight's chin.

"Drop that gun, Lillian or I'll kill you both."

Lillian began to cry. "Why did you push him out of the way? I wanted to save you."

Dwight held out a hand and then lowered it, gesturing for Lillian to drop her weapon.

"Put it down," he said, then he looked at Tanner with wet, pleading eyes. "Please don't kill her, don't kill my wife."

Several people came out of nearby homes and Tanner spotted one woman talking on the phone, no doubt calling the cops. He stared at Lillian through the hole in the window.

"Drop it!"

Lillian startled from the sound of his raised voice and released the gun. It clattered to the ground and Tanner told her to walk toward the front door. He met her there with his shotgun still pointed at Dwight, then watched as the two of them embraced.

Dwight looked at him. "What are you going to do?"

Tanner lowered the shotgun. "I'm going to kill Rossetti, for both of us."

A vehicle came to a squealing halt out front and Tanner nearly blasted it, but then he saw Cindy and Billy giving him worried looks.

Tanner left the house. "Goodbye, Dwight."

Cindy slid over and Tanner climbed into the passenger seat, as a siren could be heard approaching from the west.

Billy sped off, while Cindy gasped and touched Tanner's back. When she moved her hand into sight again, he saw that her fingers were red.

"You were shot?"

He nodded. "Grazed by a ricochet. Rossetti should hire Lillian Sorrell to kill me. She might get the job done."

"Where to?" Billy said, but Tanner ignored the question and asked Billy one of his own.

"Why did you come back?"

"We were in the donut shop across the street when I saw that woman run this way with a gun in her hand. I figured that couldn't be good."

"You were right."

"So, where to?"

"Just drive around these back streets for now, while I look for a place to lie low."

Cindy smiled at him. “It looks like you’re stuck with us again.”

And although it was against his nature, Tanner smiled back.

23
NO IFS, ANDS, OR BUTS

MERLE AND EARL CARTER WERE IN THE BASEMENT OF A home on Stewart Avenue in Las Vegas.

In particular, they were in a back corner, where a soundproof room had been constructed. There was a metal pole in the center of the room that stretched from floor to ceiling, with a drain to the right of it, and Merle took note that the drain cover was tinged a dark red.

Albert Rossetti stood just inside the doorway staring at the two brothers, while Ramone leaned against one wall with a baseball bat. The wooden bat also had flecks of color on it, dark brown splotches that looked like dried blood.

There was another man there, but Merle hadn't caught his name. The man was short, but he looked strong. When he had taken hold of Merle's wrist to handcuff him to the pole, Merle had felt his carpal bones grind together.

Once they had been secured to the pole with handcuffs, Ramone told them to sit on the floor. After they sat, Rossetti waddled over and glared down at them.

"I don't know you two. What's your game?"

Merle swallowed hard and felt his mouth go dry. When he spoke to Rossetti, he barely recognized his own voice.

"We, we was in California, in LA, and heard about the reward for Tanner, so we came here to look for him."

"You don't sound like you're from LA."

"Oh, me and Earl travel around a lot and ah, we saw your nephew once, Johnny R? We used to bring cars to his chop shop."

Ramone laughed. "They're a couple of cheap hustlers. I told you that ten G's would bring them out."

Rossetti gave the brothers a sour look. "Explain to me how Tanner got away but you're still breathing."

Merle attempted to look sincere as he repeated the lie Tanner told him to say.

"Tanner had help; some dudes that work for a guy named Hank O'Grady. They say O'Grady wants fifty grand for Tanner."

Rossetti's face screwed up as he looked over at Ramone. "Who the fuck is Hank O'Grady?"

"I never heard of him," Ramone said.

Rossetti pointed at Merle. "Are you fucking with me?"

Merle opened his mouth to answer and nothing came out.

That son of a bitch Tanner had made it sound like all they had to do was mention O'Grady's name and everything would be all right, but Rossetti looked more pissed than ever.

"Colorado!" Earl shouted. It startled Merle so much that he felt his bladder let loose a squirt. "Hank O'Grady is some big shot from Colorado and, and the guys that took Tanner said that they'd contact you soon about tradin' Tanner for the money."

Rossetti's face screwed up again. Merle thought it made him look like a confused frog.

"Some sheep fucker from Colorado thinks he can shake me down? Ramone, do we have people in Colorado?"

"Nah, but we know people that know people in Colorado. Do you want me to find out about this O'Grady?"

"Yeah, do that."

"And what about these two?"

Ramone asked the question while gesturing with the bat. Merle and Earl made soft whining noises in their throats.

Rossetti threw his chins at the short man. "Vinny here can keep an eye on them while we check things out."

"And what about losing Tanner? Do you want me to tune them up for that?"

Rossetti stared at the brothers for several seconds, but it felt like hours to Merle and Earl.

"We'll just keep them on ice for now, but if this Hank O'Grady story turns out to be bullshit, it'll be the last lie they tell."

Vinny opened the door and Rossetti and Ramone walked out of the room with him and up the stairs, leaving Merle and Earl alone.

Earl whispered to his brother. "What happens if Tanner's story about O'Grady doesn't check out?"

Merle gazed about the stark room and noticed that the walls and ceiling were also stained with blood.

"We die, Earl. That's what happens. We die."

SARA LEARNED OF THE SHOOTING INCIDENT AT THE Sorrells' home and went there to question them about Tanner, but when she and Garner arrived they found the couple in their driveway, loading Dwight's suitcases into Lillian's car.

"Are you going on a trip, Dwight?"

Dwight looked up, blinked rapidly several times and then sighed. "Agent Blake, why are you here?"

Sara pointed over at the boarded-up office window. "Someone fired shots into your house. Was that someone Tanner?"

Lillian wiped at her eyes and it caught Sara's attention.

"Mrs. Sorrell, is there something you'd like to tell us?"

Lillian shook her head and kept her mouth shut, just as she had when the police arrived, and Dwight sent them away with a lame story about a gun going off by accident.

Dwight stepped in front of his wife and closer to Sara.

"Why are you harassing me? I told you months ago that I had no connection to Tanner."

"Yes, you did, but I later found out that wasn't true. Now there's a rumor that you're also connected to Albert Rossetti somehow."

"I'm just a real estate agent."

Sara moved closer and invaded Dwight's personal space. "Tanner is still alive, isn't he? He's alive and he tried to kill you."

Dwight laughed in her face and Sara took a step backwards.

"What the hell is so funny?"

Dwight smiled. "If Tanner wanted to kill me, I'd be dead, no ifs, ands, or buts."

Sara knew Dwight spoke the truth, and once again wondered if Tanner was dead.

24
TEMPTATION

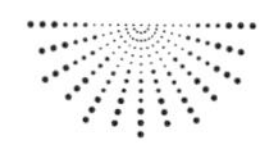

AFTER SPOTTING AN OLD HOUSE WITH A PILE OF newspapers lying atop its porch, Tanner told Billy to back the pickup down the driveway. Afterwards, he proceeded to break in the home's back door, to find the house devoid of its owners.

On a kitchen wall was a calendar with the current week circled and the word VACATION written inside it.

There was an old motor home at the bottom of the slanted driveway, and after confirming that it was drivable, Tanner gave Billy the chore of ditching the pickup. He told him to park it at least two miles away, wipe it down, and then travel back to the house on foot.

That left Tanner alone with Cindy, and as she hovered over him while cleaning his wound, he felt his desire for her rising again.

They were upstairs in the master bedroom. Tanner was shirtless and sitting on the bed, as Cindy wiped at the bullet scrape with a cotton swab. The wound was on his back, just behind his right shoulder, and Cindy was on her knees behind him as she worked.

When he had removed his shirt, her eyes had taken inventory of his earlier scars and his fresher bruises, before her fingers felt along the marks of former battles.

"This puckered scar here on your chest, is that a bullet wound?"

"Yes, from years ago."

"How bad was it?"

"I nearly died."

Concern had clouded her lovely face at those words and she began ministering to his newest wound.

Her touch was gentle, her breath warm and sweet upon his skin, and her breasts brushed against him now and then. When she leaned over, her long blonde hair would fall forward, framing her beautiful face, while blanketing his naked chest.

Cindy shifted, and once again, Tanner felt the firm breasts rub against him.

He turned his head, locking eyes with her, and saw the breath catch in her throat.

Tanner kept staring, as he searched for lustful intention, but found only a sense of girlish excitement in her blue eyes.

Cindy blushed, returned Tanner's stare, then gave a little shrug with one shoulder.

"I'm with Billy, Tanner; he's my guy."

Tanner faced forward again, breaking eye contact, and Cindy finished cleaning the wound, before placing a bandage over it.

When he stood, she got off the bed as well, and Tanner thanked her for helping him.

She smiled. "We're friends."

"Yes," he said, and put on the clean shirt he had taken from the closet.

The man of the house was bigger than Tanner in the

waist and of shorter stature, but when he tightened his belt, the pants stayed up and the height of the cuffs didn't look too bad, not with the boots he was wearing. The dark suit coat was large, but that too worked out, as it hid the gun tucked in his waistband.

Cindy made a stack of sandwiches while they waited for Billy to return, but then she received a call from him instead.

"Where are you?"

"Put the speakerphone on, I need to talk to Tanner too."

Cindy hit a button and Tanner heard traffic sounds in the background.

"What's up, Billy?"

"Oh man, we've got a problem. I was two blocks from the house when I saw a bunch of pickup trucks by the park here. I recognized some of these guys, and Cindy, I saw your dad."

"Daddy's here?"

"Yeah, and it looks like they're getting ready to attack, like they're planning the best way to do it."

"Are you on this side of the park?" Tanner said.

"Yeah."

"Go to the other side and we'll pick you up in the motor home."

"Tanner."

"Yeah?"

"Take care of Cindy, man, okay?"

"She'll stay safe, now get going and we'll see you."

Tanner ended the call, then he stared at the phone in his hand.

"How long have you had this phone?"

"About a year, why?"

"It's how they found us. They must have a man watching the house too."

Cindy spun around and stared at the kitchen windows. "What do we do?"

Tanner handed her the Glock he had taken from one of Aldo's men.

"There's a round in the chamber. If anyone tries to hurt you, aim at their chest and squeeze the trigger."

Cindy looked down at the gun in her hand and then up at Tanner.

"Isn't there a safety switch on it somewhere?"

"It's built into the trigger."

"Where are you going?"

"There's likely at least one spotter outside, someone to peek in windows and try to figure out how many people are inside. I'm going out to take care of them. You stay here, and when you hear the motor home start, come outside."

"Be careful, Tanner."

"Right."

Edwin "Buck" Seevers had worked as a bartender for over a year and had tangled and tussled with his share of mean drunks, but he never had to use a gun on any of them. It felt odd to be carrying one.

Buck considered himself an actor. He had done several plays and worked the dinner theater circuit in Colorado. Buck was saving enough to move to Los Angeles next year, which is why he came along with the others to Vegas.

He was getting an extra thousand for what should be one day's work. If tips stayed good and he was frugal, he hoped to be in LA in six months.

Buck was outside the kitchen window of the home Tanner was using. He could hear voices, but couldn't make out what they were saying. Still, it sounded like one was male and the other female. Since the signal from the phone was coming from inside, he assumed it was the girl and one of her abductors.

He was just about to call the rest of his group and tell them it was a go, when Tanner snuck up from behind and blasted him with a stun gun.

Buck fell to his knees and Tanner jammed the Mossberg against his side.

"How many are you?"

Buck couldn't answer right away, as he was too busy drooling from the blast, but when his mind cleared, he stuttered out an answer.

"There's, there's, twelve, twelve of us, thirteen if you count the girl's father."

Tanner ground the shotgun into Buck's ribs. "Did they bring the money?"

"Yeah, just in case."

"Give me your phone."

Buck handed over his cell phone and Tanner shut it off. When there was time, he'd remove the battery.

He told Buck to get on his feet and marched him into the motor home, where he gave him another blast from the stun gun, before starting the engine.

As Tanner waited for Cindy to join him, he gave Buck a third blast and then used strips of fabric to bind Buck's wrists and ankles. The material had been torn from the window curtains hanging over the vehicle's tiny sink.

Cindy appeared, holding the gun by its barrel like a club, and her eyes grew wide when she saw Tanner tying up Buck.

"He works for Mr. O'Grady. I've seen him around town."

"Yes, and he'll come in handy."

Buck recovered again, and after shaking his head, he spoke. He used the voice he always used when he performed in Guys and Dolls, as he tried to sound tough.

"Mr. O'Grady isn't someone you want to fuck with, dude."

Cindy walked over and stared down at him. "This is Tanner, and you don't want to fuck with him."

Buck stared at her in shock, then at Tanner, and decided to keep his mouth shut.

Seconds later, they were on their way out of the driveway.

Cindy held out the gun for Tanner to take back and he told her to keep it.

"Really?"

"Yes, you may need it someday."

"Tanner?"

"Yeah?"

"Thanks for helping us like this."

"What are friends for?" Tanner said.

And then the two of them went to pick up Billy.

25
THE HEART WANTS WHAT IT WANTS

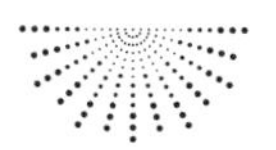

HANK O'GRADY WATCHED HIS SON ENTER HIS OFFICE AND knew just what was on Ricky's mind.

It was Cindy, Cindy Preston. She was the only thing the kid had thought about since coming home from college and discovering that the cute girl had blossomed into a sex kitten.

Ricky took a seat on the corner of the desk. He was twenty-three, good-looking, and spoiled rotten. Cindy's rejection of his advances had only made him want her more, and he was convinced that he loved her and that they were meant to be man and wife.

When at home, Ricky was treated like a prince. The youngest of two children, he was O'Grady's only son. O'Grady had always given Ricky anything he wanted, and he was determined that Cindy would not be an exception.

Ricky had cost his old man a small fortune over the years, as O'Grady had paid to cover up his son's indiscretions or fulfill his desires. Ricky's obsession with Cindy was proving to be expensive as well.

"Any news?"

"Yeah, I just heard back from Rossetti's man, some dude named Ramone. He's going to meet with Joe Preston and hand over Billy and Cindy."

"It's like a kidnapping?"

O'Grady stroked his chin. "I hadn't looked at it that way, but yeah, you're right."

"Are they flying back tonight?"

"I have the pilot standing by in Vegas."

"I should have gone with them."

O'Grady shook his head. "It might get dangerous out there and I'm not putting you in harm's way."

Ricky stood. There was concern showing on his young face. "Nothing bad better happen to Cindy."

"It won't. I meant that the trouble would start after we get her back, that's when the boys are going to teach that Rossetti a hard lesson."

Ricky paced about the room, his eyes bright.

"I can't wait to see Cindy again. And this time she'll come around, I know she will, and then we'll marry."

O'Grady smiled, pleased to see his son happy. "Once you marry that girl, I want grandsons."

Ricky stopped pacing and stared at his father; he then walked over and leaned across the desk.

"What's to stop Cindy from running away again? She might go off looking for Billy, or he might come back here."

"That's not going to happen, because it won't be possible."

"What do you mean?"

O'Grady waved off the question, thinking that Ricky was too young or too weak to hear the truth, but then he reconsidered.

"Listen, boy, you'll be running this ranch someday, so

you might as well know something right now; sometimes you have to play for keeps, do you get me?"

Ricky straightened, as his eyebrows went up in surprise.

"You're going to have Billy killed?"

"Yeah, accident or not, the boy stabbed you; he doesn't get to live after that."

"Are they bringing him back here?"

"No, Joe Preston will probably drive his ass out into the Nevada desert and put a bullet in his brain."

"Too bad," Ricky said, his eyes narrowing in hate. "If Billy came back here, I'd kill him myself."

O'Grady beamed at his son. The kid had grit after all, and he realized that the ranch would someday be in safe hands.

26
IT DOESN'T WORK THAT WAY

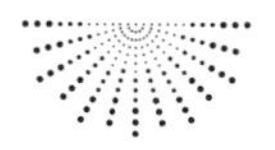

TANNER HAD CINDY REMOVE THE BATTERY FROM HER phone, but kept the device, as he could later use it as bait.

Buck turned out to be personable, at least as far as Billy and Cindy were concerned. He kept them laughing as he told them stories about the theater and the acting life.

Tanner had even released him from his bonds. Buck was no threat, of that he was sure, and was equally certain that Billy could handle him if he tried anything. Tanner also promised Buck that if he caused him grief he would kill him. He saw by the man's reaction that he was believed.

They were in a Walmart parking lot. Tanner had sent Billy and Cindy into the store to buy a few pay-as-you-go phones, along with other items and food.

Tanner had already used one of the phones to call Hank O'Grady and set up a meet with Joe Preston, Cindy's father. O'Grady still believed that Tanner was Ramone and that he was going to trade him Billy and Cindy for fifty thousand dollars, but Tanner had other plans, and other calls to make.

As Buck began one more tale, Tanner left the trio to talk, while he went to the rear of the motor home. After sliding closed the bedroom door, Tanner called the number that was in the envelope Dwight had passed along.

His call was answered by a young woman who Tanner thought sounded hot, but snooty.

"Good afternoon and whom may I say is calling?"

"Tanner."

"Please hold."

She was gone for just over a minute, then she informed Tanner that someone would be calling him back on the phone he was using within the next few minutes.

Tanner ended the first call and waited for the return call to come in.

The sound of laughter drifted in from the front of the motor home as Buck continued to amuse Billy and Cindy.

Tanner sighed. If he kept picking up strays, he'd soon need a rooming house in which to board them.

The phone rang. Tanner answered it and said four words. "You wanted to talk?"

The voice that replied had a quality to it that spoke of money and power.

"Tanner, this is Frank Richards. While this line is secure, I would like to meet with you in person."

"Are you in New York?"

"I'm in Las Vegas. I flew here to handle this problem."

Tanner gave Frank Richards the location of the Walmart and told him that he would meet him inside, at the garden center.

"I can be there in half an hour. I'll bring two men along, but I assure you, I only want to talk."

"I understand," Tanner said.

He had no concern about a hit or being grabbed up, at least not while Richards was present. Frank Richards managed people and incidents, but he didn't do the work himself.

If he had decided to have Tanner hit, he would send someone to do it, but he would never be near when it happened. Not in as public a place as a Walmart. Being personally involved with a hit would go against Richards' breeding and he would find violence distasteful, although he regularly ordered that violence be done to others.

The call ended and Tanner informed Billy and Cindy that he would be meeting someone inside the store, he then stared at Buck.

"You're going to behave while I'm gone."

It was a statement, not a question.

Buck held up his hands to the level of his shoulders.

"I'm not a tough guy, Tanner. I just joined O'Grady's posse for the thousand bucks it paid. I was also told that Cindy was being held hostage."

"He's cool," Billy said, and Cindy nodded in agreement.

Tanner told them he would be back before an hour passed and then left the motor home and walked to the store's entrance, where he stood and watched for Frank Richards' arrival.

Frank Richards was not a mobster, not in the traditional sense. He was a businessman with deep corporate ties and a key member of the Conglomerate.

The Conglomerate's members were Italian, Irish, Russian, African, and increasingly, Wasp, as people like Frank Richards influenced recruitment.

Tanner wasn't a member of the Conglomerate, nor of anything else, although many of his contracts came through them and he had been asked to join them, but always declined. Tanner was a loner, a professional, and the best killer money could buy. He had been trained to be such by his mentor, Tanner Six. Tanner was the seventh in a line of assassins who passed down their knowledge and skills.

Richards' limo appeared, and the man himself got out of it with two bodyguards. The bodyguards were both big men, but hardly what might be termed gorillas.

Tanner knew one of them by his first name, which was Gary, but he had never seen the other man before.

Tanner walked behind a large display of diapers and waited for the trio to pass, then he followed them to the garden department by walking parallel to them along another aisle.

As the three men entered the garden area and turned right, Tanner entered and turned left, to meet them at the rear by the fence, near a large stack of potting soil.

As the bodyguards' eyes fell upon him, Tanner spread his hands and revealed them to be empty.

Richards greeted him with a nod and moved closer. It was a weekday, and although the garden department had a steady flow of customers milling about, they were far enough away to be able to speak in a normal voice.

"Your time in prison has left you thinner, Tanner; although I see the work detail on that building site gave you ample opportunity to get some sun."

Tanner nodded. Richards was telling him he had kept tabs on him while he was in prison, or else how would he know about the work detail at the construction site? Tanner wondered if Richards had made certain he was on that detail and if so, why?

Would he want him outside prison walls so it would be easier to escape, or so that it would have made Tanner easier to kill? If the latter, it would explain why he was attacked for no apparent reason while working on the site.

"You wanted to talk, let's talk."

"Very well, I want you to leave Rossetti be. I know I engaged you to... do what you do, but things have changed in our relationship since that time and Albert Rossetti is off-limits and under the Conglomerate's protection."

"You paid me to kill him and that's just what I'm going to do."

Tanner saw Richards wince when he used the word "kill" as if not actually saying it made the act nicer.

Richards leaned closer and Tanner could detect the aftershave on the man even over the earthiness of the potting soil. It was a scent like Bay Rum, but richer. He filed the odor away in case Richards ever became a target, because you never knew what might give your quarry's location away.

"If you harm Rossetti I'll be forced to act against you, and Tanner, you are not the only one with your particular set of skills."

"You mean you'll send someone to kill me? Do that, and you'll not only have lost Rossetti, but also whoever you send."

Richards let out a long breath, while appearing to be annoyed, and perhaps surprised. He wasn't a man used to hearing the word, "No."

"I hired you, Tanner, and now I'm telling you to stand down. Rossetti is no longer a target. You can keep the money, that's not a problem, but if anything happens to Rossetti, I assure you, the same fate will befall you."

"Richards, I kill people and I never fail to take out a target once money has changed hands. There's no off switch. It doesn't work that way. Once I'm switched on, I'm on, and whoever I'm after will die."

Richards had turned red while Tanner was talking. When he spoke again, it was through gritted teeth. "You'll do as I say, or you'll die. Is that simple enough for you, Tanner?"

"We're done here," Tanner said. "Now leave."

"What?"

"You heard me, Richards. You wanted to talk, we talked, now go away. I've got work to do."

Richards' mouth dropped open and he sent forth an astonished laugh.

"You must be insane. You think you can talk to me that way?"

Tanner ignored the question, it was stupid, and he had been eyeing Richards' bodyguards as the man talked. The one named Gary had slid his hand closer to the holster on his belt. Tanner caught the man's eye. Gary held his gaze for a second, and his hand froze where it was.

"What do you want us to do, Mr. Richards?" Gary asked.

Richards flicked a glance at Gary, looked around at the nearby shoppers, and let out a long slow breath.

"I want to leave here and never see this man again," Richards said. He spun around and stalked off, with Gary at his side, and the other bodyguard walking sideways and eyeing Tanner.

When they were out of sight, Tanner climbed up on the stack of potting soil and went over the fence. He landed on the balls of his feet, while steadying himself with the palm of one hand.

Afterwards, he climbed back into the motor home, which was parked twenty yards away.

After returning the greetings of his companions, Tanner started the massive vehicle and headed for the exit.

As he drove around the corner of the building, he saw that a black SUV had joined the limousine, and that four men were talking to the limo driver.

Tanner halted and watched as Richards appeared and pointed back at the building. He then saw two of the new men go inside, while the other two stayed in front of the store.

Tanner drove on. When he reached the exit for the parking lot, Richards' limo was behind them. They stayed in tandem for two blocks, then Tanner turned left, while the limo went right.

Cindy joined him up front and sat beside him in the RV's other Captain's seat.

"How did the meeting go?"

Tanner nodded. "Just as I expected."

27
IT'S TIME TO GET PAID

Ramone walked into Rossetti's office and saw an open briefcase full of cash.

"You giving me a bonus, Boss?"

"You wish, no, that's the money O'Grady wants for Tanner."

"About that, I got news."

"Yeah?"

"I talked to a guy in Denver, Al Rivers, he runs the sports book up there and he filled me in on O'Grady. The dude owns some big ranch and there's a town named O'Grady too, but it's a small place and everyone in it works on the ranch."

"It's like a company town, hmm?"

"Yeah, O'Grady owns the whorehouse, controls the gambling, and sells weed, but it's small-time shit. Rivers said they looked at it a few years ago and decided it wasn't worth their trouble, plus, the place is in the middle of nowhere."

Rossetti stood from behind his desk and paced.

"This guy O'Grady stumbles across Tanner, sees a

chance to make an easy fifty K, and puts the squeeze on me. I'll tell you something, Ramone, once we take care of Tanner, I'm gonna teach O'Grady some respect."

"There's one more thing."

"What's that?"

"O'Grady sent some troops here; Rivers says maybe a dozen."

"He can't be thinking of going to war with us, can he?"

Ramone shrugged.

Joy appeared and gave a tentative knock on the open door. Rossetti glared at her.

"What?"

"There's a man on the phone. He says that he works for someone named O'Grady?"

Rossetti looked down at his desk and saw a light blinking on the phone. He waved Joy off with a sweeping motion of his hand. When she was gone, he spoke to Ramone.

"This must be the call to set up the swap."

Rossetti picked up the receiver and stabbed the blinking button with a stubby finger.

"Talk to me."

Miles away, Buck took a deep breath and prepared to play his part. Buck told himself just to think of it as playing a role, a part in a play. Tanner had coached him on how to react and what to say and he was more than ready to do it, because he figured if he shined in his role that Tanner would let him have a return engagement with life, instead of closing the curtains forever.

Tanner could have made the call himself and changed his voice, but he hadn't wanted to risk having his voice recognized by Rossetti or Ramone. By using Buck, it also gave Tanner an opportunity to evaluate Buck, and judge if he was trustworthy.

Buck was seated at the fold-down table inside the motor home with Cindy, Billy, and Tanner.

Tanner had the Mossberg lying atop the table with the barrel pointed in Buck's direction. Sitting in the middle of the table was a cell phone on speaker mode.

A clicking sound came from the phone, then a deep voice made a demand.

"Talk to me."

Buck let out a breath and began his role. "Rossetti, this is Joe Preston. I'm Mr. O'Grady's foreman and I'm ready to hand over Tanner. Do you have the money?"

"I got it."

"Fifty grand?"

"Yeah, goddamn it, I said it was ready, didn't I?"

"Calm down, fat man, this is just business. There's no need to get excited."

The phone was silent, but Buck could feel a sense of malice emanating from it. When Rossetti spoke again, it sounded like he was doing it through gritted teeth.

"Let me talk with Tanner."

"He's here, hold on."

Across the table, Tanner let several beats pass before speaking.

"Rossetti?"

"It's me, Tanner, and I'm about to get my hands on you."

"Screw you."

"Yeah, I got plans for you, tough guy, and let me tell you, you're not going to like them one bit. Preston?"

"I'm here," Buck said. "Are you ready to meet?"

"When and where?"

Buck gave Rossetti the name of a nearby mall.

"That's kind of public, isn't it?"

"That's the whole idea. I'll bring Tanner, your man brings the cash, we make the trade, and no one gets hurt. Got it?"

"One man each?"

"That's right?"

"How is one man gonna handle Tanner?"

"Don't worry; we're going to juice him up with an animal tranquilizer, just enough to make him nice and tame. People will think he's a happy drunk."

"I know you have more men here."

"We do. They'll be ready to bring the hellfire down on that house of yours if I don't call and tell them the switch happened without any grief, capeesh, paisan?"

"All right, one man each at the damn mall, but when?"

"Thirty minutes."

"That's crazy; we'll need time to—"

"You heard me, Rossetti. Now do as you're told."

And with those words, Tanner reached over and ended the call. He looked at Buck.

"Not bad."

"You're really going to let me go after the switch?" Buck said.

"I'll let you go, but not until later, if I let you go too early you might warn O'Grady."

Buck made a face. "To hell with O'Grady. I'm not going back. I've always wanted to go to Hollywood, and once I survive this, I'm going. I'll be just another starving actor, but I'm going anyway."

Tanner grabbed the Mossberg and stood.

"It's time to get paid."

~

Back at Rossetti's, Ramone watched a purple vein pulse at his boss's temple and was glad that he was neither Tanner nor O'Grady.

"Go to the mall and get Tanner."

"I will, but we need more guys here in case O'Grady makes a move."

"I'll take care of that while you're getting Tanner."

"Those two from this morning, the Carter brothers, they're not much, but they're a couple of more bodies."

"Yeah, I'll tell Vinny to let them go and send them here. Once you have Tanner, take him to Vinny, but let Vinny know that Tanner is a handful."

Ramone shut the briefcase and picked up the money.

"I better get a move on. The damn mall is a hike."

"Ramone?"

"Yeah?"

"Don't get fancy. Just make the trade and we'll deal with O'Grady later."

"I guess we're going to war, huh?"

Rossetti sneered. "O'Grady is gonna wish he never heard of me."

Ramone left with the briefcase in hand and Rossetti picked up his phone. It was time to bring in the troops.

28
THE ILLUSION OF SECURITY

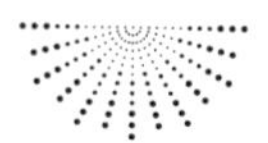

RAMONE WALKED TOWARD TANNER AND BUCK AMID THE crowds in the mall. He grinned when he saw that Tanner's hands were behind his back, and likely bound together beneath the suit jacket draped across his shoulders.

He figured that Buck was Preston, the man Rossetti had spoken to on the phone, and thought that he was unimpressive in person. It wasn't until he stood before them that he noticed Buck was sweating and that Tanner looked calm.

Ramone stared at Buck. "We had a deal, Preston."

Tanner moved his hands around to the front and Ramone saw that he was palming a small gun.

"What the hell is this?"

Tanner spoke to Buck. "Get the briefcase and hand him the phone."

Buck stuck out a hand. With a loud sigh, Ramone handed over the money, while taking the cell phone, Cindy's cell phone.

"What's this phone for?"

"There's one number in the address book. It belongs to

O'Grady. He's willing to stand down if Rossetti pays him a million."

"A million?" Ramone said, and spoke the words so loudly that the people passing by them stared at him in shock. Ramone calmed himself and spoke to Buck.

"Preston, Rossetti is going to roast your balls for this. Why are you assholes helping Tanner?"

"I outbid Rossetti for my life," Tanner said. "And I'm also paying O'Grady to help me take down your boss. The million bucks would be enough for him and he'd tell his men to walk away, but I won't, I'll just keep coming until Rossetti is dead."

Ramone stared at Tanner in disbelief and asked a question.

"Can I walk out of here, or are you planning to waste me in front of all these people?"

"I'll let you do what you do best—play errand boy. Go back to Rossetti and tell him I'm coming for him; I'm coming for him and I won't be alone."

"Damn it, Tanner, none of this shit is even necessary anymore. The contract on Rossetti was cancelled while you were in prison. Walk away. Walk away and maybe I can get Al to call a truce."

"I was paid to kill Rossetti and I never fail on a contract."

"You're a fool."

"Leave, Ramone. If you're smart, you won't be anywhere near Rossetti when I come for him."

Ramone gave Tanner a look of disgust, then spun around and marched off.

Buck let out a gasp. "Shit, Tanner. My heart's beating a mile a second."

"We're not done yet, so calm down."

"Oh Christ, what's next?"

"Now it's time to shakedown O'Grady," Tanner said.

He pulled Buck along by the arm and into a clothing shop, where he walked through the back room to shouts of protest from the woman who managed the store.

"Hey! You two can't just walk back in here. Who are you?"

Tanner ignored her and grabbed two mannequins, which he passed to Buck. After taking a roll of money from a side pocket, he peeled off a few hundreds and placed them atop a stack of boxes.

The woman looked on in confusion, but when Tanner and Buck headed for the rear door where deliveries were received, she shouted at them again.

"I'll call security!"

"There's no such thing in this world," Tanner told her. He opened the door, held it for Buck to pass through, then climbed aboard the waiting motor home, with fifty thousand dollars of Rossetti's money.

29

GANG RAPE IS ICKY

Tanner instructed Billy to drive the motor home around to the other end of the mall and park.

This time, Cindy was accompanying Tanner and Buck, as they went to meet with her father.

Tanner spoke to Billy.

"You remember where to pick us up?"

"Yeah and I'll be there, don't worry."

Tanner wasn't worried. He was leaving the kid alone with fifty grand in a briefcase, but he figured Billy would never leave Cindy behind, even if the cash tempted him.

The trio left the motor home and headed for the nearest entrance. Cindy was dressed in an oversized hoodie that hid most of her face, along with a pair of loose cargo pants, which Tanner hoped would disguise her shapely figure.

They had bought these items before scheduling the meet, and it was Cindy's job to alert Tanner if she spotted anyone she recognized other than her father.

Buck had told Tanner that O'Grady had ordered

Preston to hand over the money, get Cindy back, and then stay out of the way while the other men attacked Rossetti.

O'Grady's men had orders to follow wherever Cindy's cell phone signal led them. If that were true, then O'Grady's men were following Ramone straight back to Rossetti's, since Tanner had given Ramone Cindy's phone.

Cindy trailed along behind Tanner and Buck, while scrutinizing the faces around them. She had lived on the ranch her entire life and would recognize anyone from the ranch or the nearby town. However, the only familiar face she saw was that of her father, who stood in front of an ice cream parlor, holding a briefcase and looking fearful and out of place.

BUCK SPOKE TO PRESTON AND TANNER COULD TELL THAT the man recognized him.

"Mr. Preston, this is Ramone, he works for Mr. Rossetti."

"Why are you with him, Buck, have you switched sides?"

Buck feigned anger.

"Hell no, but they caught me snooping around that house where they were holding Cindy and captured me."

"You've seen Cindy? Is she all right?"

"Yeah, she's good."

"Rossetti's men haven't… touched her. I'm not sure that Mr. O'Grady's son would still want her if she were soiled that way."

Buck glared at Preston, his disgust plain to see.

"She hasn't been raped, and I don't think she gives a damn what Ricky O'Grady thinks of her."

Preston made a show of checking his watch before

speaking to Tanner.

"You're late, and where is Cindy? I thought we were making a trade? I've got the money right here."

As he mentioned the money, Tanner revealed the gun in his waistband, which was beneath his suit coat.

"Hand that over, pass it to Buck."

"Where's Cindy?"

"The money, Preston, or you'll never see Cindy again."

Preston hesitated, but then he handed Buck the briefcase.

Tanner smiled. "There's been a change of plans. Mr. Rossetti has decided that a million dollars would be a fairer price for Cindy."

Preston looked at Tanner as if he were crazy. "What? No. O'Grady won't pay that, not even to please his son, and he'll be furious at losing the money in that briefcase. Ramone, you don't know O'Grady, the man… he'll attack you. Tell him, Buck, tell him about the attack."

"I already did, Mr. Preston; he threatened to kill me if I didn't talk."

"I can stop it. Give me back the money, my daughter, and that boy Billy too, and I promise you I'll get Mr. O'Grady to calm down."

Tanner sighed. "Mr. Rossetti asked me to give you a message to take to Mr. O'Grady."

"What is it, a way to end this?"

"Not exactly, he wants you to tell O'Grady to go fuck himself and that if he tries anything other than paying the million, he'll kill him."

Preston reached for the briefcase in desperation and Tanner pressed a hand against his chest.

"Don't be stupid. Just turn around and walk away."

Preston stood there, his mouth open in shock. Then, he asked Buck a question.

"How many men are guarding Rossetti?"

"Six," Buck blurted out, before Tanner gave him a sharp look.

Preston smiled. "All right, if it's a war you want, you got it. Come on, Buck, we're going."

"He stays with me," Tanner said. "He'll be one less gun in the fight."

Preston accepted that logic, sent Buck an apologetic glance, and walked away.

Buck spoke to Tanner as they watched him leave.

"How'd I do?"

"Good, if they think Rossetti only has six men guarding him they'll get overconfident."

Cindy joined them, and Tanner saw that tears had formed in her eyes, but had yet to fall.

"Did he ask about me?"

"In a way," Tanner said. "He was worried that you might have been gang raped by Rossetti's men and become soiled and unacceptable for O'Grady's son."

That made the tears flow, and Cindy brushed them away.

"Bastard."

Tanner handed her the briefcase. "That's money for a new start, paid for by O'Grady."

"You're letting Billy and I keep this?"

"Yes."

Cindy shed more tears, but their source was not one of sorrow. She stood on her toes and kissed Tanner on the lips.

"Thank you."

Tanner started walking toward the exit where Billy was waiting.

"Let's get out of here. I don't want to be late for the war."

30
HARD WHERE IT COUNTS, SOFT WHERE IT MATTERS

Sara spoke to the FBI agent in Colorado and learned that over a dozen of O'Grady's men had boarded a private jet bound for Vegas.

That news puzzled her, but then she learned that O'Grady was in some sort of dispute with Rossetti, and she wondered if a gang war was in the making.

Garner shook his head in confusion. "What the hell would those two be fighting over? Their turfs are nearly a thousand miles apart."

Sara thought about it. When she came up with an answer, a wide grin covered her face.

"It's Tanner. The bastard is starting a war between those two as a distraction. That's why he saved those kids from O'Grady's men. He's using them as some sort of lure for O'Grady and probably blaming everything on Rossetti, while Rossetti thinks that O'Grady is giving him grief."

"Are you serious? Is Tanner that devious?"

"Oh, you have no idea what that man is capable of."

"So, this also means he's still alive, but what should we do about this?"

Sara stood. "I'm going to camp out at Rossetti's and wait for the fireworks to begin. Once they do, I'll know Tanner is on the scene."

Garner grabbed his jacket off the back of the chair. "You know, we could defuse this by warning either Rossetti or O'Grady. We'd save a few of their men's lives in the bargain."

Sara moved closer to Garner.

"That might cause Tanner to hit Rossetti somewhere else other than his home. If that happened, Tanner might slip away."

"We're talking lives here, Sara."

"I thought we were partners, Jake?"

"We are, but we're also talking about slaughter. O'Grady sent a dozen men and Rossetti will have at least that many. If they go at each other it will be brutal."

"They'll be thugs killing thugs, who cares?"

"Their families care, and maybe innocents will get hurt, like that girl, Joy."

"Rossetti's whore? I think she's far from innocent."

"You know what I mean?"

Sara took several steps toward the elevator, then looked back at Garner.

"Are you coming?"

"No."

"Will you warn Rossetti?"

"I… I don't know."

"Let it be, Garner," Sara said.

She walked over and pressed the elevator button, then stepped on when the doors slid aside. Just before the doors closed, she saw Garner staring at her with a face contorted by indecision.

Sara sighed. Who knew the stud had a soft heart?

31
STRESS IS A KILLER

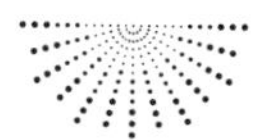

AFTER GIVING ROSSETTI THE NEWS OF TANNER AND O'Grady's seeming alliance, Ramone feared for his life, as he saw the murderous glint in his boss's eyes.

"You just gave him the money without a fight?"

Ramone spread his hands in a gesture of helplessness.

"We were in the middle of a crowd of shoppers. If I went for my gun it would have been on the news, and then we'd have all kind of heat come down on us."

"Fifty fucking thousand dollars and Tanner is still out there."

"He's coming, and he's coming here with O'Grady's men. In fact, he had Preston with him at the mall."

Rossetti laughed, and the suddenness of it unnerved Ramone even more.

"Some Colorado cow pie thinks he can send a few troops here and I'll have a fainting spell and cough up a million. The man must be crazy. How many guys are here?"

"Besides myself, fifteen, counting those two brothers who lost Tanner to O'Grady's men."

"Place those two at the front door. When O'Grady attacks, they'll be the first ones whacked and we won't lose any good men."

"There's one more thing. That hot FBI agent is back. I spotted her watching the place from across the highway."

"Hopefully, when the shit goes down she'll get hers, useless bitch. All she cares about is catching Tanner."

"Al."

"What?"

"You can still leave. Everything is set, including the ATV."

"I'm not running, not yet, my guys will handle this."

"That's what you said about Aldo."

Rossetti groaned. "Go check on things; I need time to think."

When Ramone left the office, Rossetti went to the closet in the corner of the room and stared at the back wall, which was the entrance to his escape tunnel. It comforted him to know he could run if needed.

After pouring a glass of Scotch, he went to the window behind his desk and stared out at the pool, hoping that the sight of the blue water would soothe him.

He didn't fear O'Grady, or even Tanner, but he was not a young man anymore and he could feel the stress eating at him. He rubbed his temples in an attempt to halt the headache forming behind his eyes.

"My boys will stop Tanner," he mumbled to himself, but the words sounded as false as a promise. When he wiped his brow, his hand came away slick with sweat.

There was a knock on the door, and after Rossetti yelled, "Come in!" Joy entered the room.

"Mr. Rossetti?"

"What?"

"Can I talk to you, sir? There's something I want to ask you."

Rossetti stared at her. Joy had been out at the pool earlier and she still wore a red bikini beneath a pink silk robe, which showed off her long legs.

Rossetti took his seat, told her to close the door, and gestured her over. She was just what he needed to relieve the stress.

At the door, Joy took a deep breath knowing what was coming, but also knowing that afterwards, the fat man might be more agreeable to her request.

She smiled the practiced smile of the whore and walked over to stand in front of Rossetti.

"Get naked and suck me off," he said.

Joy removed what little she wore and dropped to her knees, to begin unzipping his pants.

As she worked on him, Rossetti reached atop the desk, removed the belt from Joy's robe, and played with the sash between his hands, enjoying the feel of the silk as she pleasured him.

The entire act took less than ten minutes, and as Rossetti sat slumped in his chair with the slack look of satisfaction on his round face, Joy decided to ask her question.

"Can I leave? I heard that there might be trouble and I don't want to get caught in the middle."

"Who said there might be trouble?"

Joy gave a little shrug. "It's just talk."

"Don't I pay you enough?" Rossetti asked.

Joy heard the anger creeping into his voice. She smiled and began massaging his limp member between her hands.

"You're very generous; it's just that I'm scared."

Rossetti narrowed his eyes and looped the sash from the robe around her neck.

"Why are you scared?"

"I heard some men were coming here to cause trouble," Joy said, and tugged at the sash, which had begun to tighten.

"Are you saying that I can't protect my turf?"

"No sir, I would never—"

"You think a bunch of clodhoppers from the Rockies can just come here and dictate to me, is that what you think?"

Joy shook her head as she tried to yank the sash free from her throat, but Rossetti had tightened it to the point that she could barely breathe.

She wheezed out words from a face that was turning red.

"Please, don't… I, I have a, a little girl."

Rossetti gnashed his teeth and pulled harder. "Is she a worthless whore like you, a fucking worthless whore who wants to run at the first sign of trouble?"

Joy's eyes bulged. She grabbed Rossetti's wrists and attempted to break his hold. He was too strong and she gave up that tactic, then hit him. When her right hand brushed his penis, she was struck by two thoughts. First, was her surprise that the violence had aroused him to hardness, and second, was that it made him vulnerable.

Joy grabbed hold of Rossetti with both hands and dug her nails into his flesh.

Rossetti let out a cry of pain and shoved her away, before standing and feeling his penis for damage. A visual check was out of the question, as his gut stuck out too far for him to see it without a mirror.

Joy ripped the belt from her throat as she gasped in air. She had made it to her hands and knees when the first kick landed.

There was an audible *CRACK!* as two ribs on her left

side broke. The pain made her roll over onto her back. Rossetti smiled, raised his foot high, and stomped down with his full force and weight on Joy's stomach. Joy screamed and doubled up in agony. That's when the foot left her midsection and collided with her chin, snapping her head back and bouncing it off the floor.

That kick was followed by more kicks that broke several teeth, her nose and her right eye socket. Every time she cried out in pain, it only enraged him more.

By the time Rossetti finished his assault, he was drenched in sweat, wheezing as if he'd run for miles, and Joy had been dead for nearly a minute.

He sent a gob of frothy spit onto the body as he spoke in a gasping breath.

"You wanted… out… you're out."

He headed for the bathroom on the right side of the room to clean up, while leaving bloody shoe prints in his wake.

32
GOODBYES

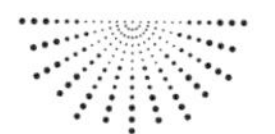

TANNER SAID GOODBYE TO BILLY AND CINDY IN THE parking lot of the Greyhound bus station on South Main Street.

They were standing outside the motor home and Billy wore a backpack with the cash inside. It was money Tanner had tricked out of Hank O'Grady.

Cindy gave him a hug and a kiss on the cheek, while Billy pumped his hand and thanked him yet again for giving them money for a fresh start.

"You have that address I gave you?"

"Yeah, Tanner, but do you really think Cindy and I need new identities?"

"It's better to be safe than sorry, and with a new ID, O'Grady will never find you. It won't be cheap though, expect to spend a good chunk of that cash."

Cindy wiped away tears. "I'll miss you, Tanner. Be careful at Rossetti's."

Tanner smiled at her. He liked Cindy, and that was something he couldn't say about many people.

"You two take care of each other, this world's a bitch."

They sent him a wave and walked off toward the entrance to the train station, which was adjacent to the bus terminal.

Tanner went back inside the motor home and stared at Buck, who was sitting at the table.

Buck swallowed hard. "You weren't lying were you, about letting me go?"

Tanner reached into his side pocket and took out a thick wad of bills. It was what was left of the money he'd taken off the pimp he killed.

He handed it to Buck and Buck took it as if it might bite him.

"You're giving me money?"

"You never got paid by O'Grady, and you did good work for me."

Buck looked down at the pile of cash. "You pay well, and this will give me a good start in L.A. Thanks."

Tanner walked over and opened the door. "Break a leg."

Buck headed down the motor home's metal steps, then looked up at Tanner.

"Thanks Tanner, and you know what, I might write a screenplay about all this someday."

Tanner shook his head. "No one would believe it."

Buck laughed at that, and then he was off with a wave.

Tanner got behind the wheel of the mammoth vehicle and headed for Rossetti's, however, he did make one stop along the way, where he bought four bags of ice from a liquor store.

With that chore done, he was back on the road, confident that he would finally fulfill his contract on Rossetti.

33

THANK GOD FOR POWER WINDOWS

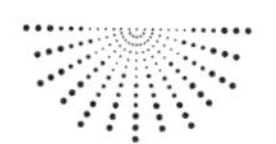

JOE PRESTON WAS SITTING ON THE SIDE OF THE BED IN A motel room with several of O'Grady's men standing around him.

He had put off making the call as long as he could, but eventually he called O'Grady, and the rancher tore him a new asshole over the phone.

"Let me get this straight. You lost a man, you gave away my money to another man, Billy Benton is still walking around, and you have no fucking idea where Cindy is. Do I have that right, Joe?"

"We know where Cindy is, we're still tracking her phone, but the thing is, she's at Rossetti's house and he has men there."

"He has men? I *have* men, or don't you remember the twelve goddamn guys I sent with you?"

"Hank, do you really want to start a war out here?"

"I want my money back. I want Billy out of the way, and I want Cindy's ass back here so I can stop hearing my son whine about her. Do what it takes, Joe, but bring that girl back here, and don't think that the money isn't coming out of your ass too."

"Hank, I—"

"Enough of you, is Drake there? Put Drake on."

Preston held up the phone and spoke to a bearded man dressed all in denim.

"He wants to speak to you."

The man took the phone with a grin on his face.

"It's me, Hank."

"The thousand-dollar bonus just became two grand each, but I want you to move on Rossetti as soon as possible. The longer you wait, the more men he'll be able to call in."

"How many guys does this Rossetti have?"

Preston overheard the question and answered.

"Buck said Rossetti had six men protecting him."

Drake rubbed a hand across his beard. "This shit could get serious, Hank. I mean, we'll probably have to shoot our way in there."

"I know that, but here's what you do. You make sure Rossetti starts things first, that way it'll be self-defense. Afterwards, we'll claim that Cindy was kidnapped and that it was a rescue mission. The man already demanded a million dollars for her, so we'll call it a ransom. If the cops get involved, blame everything on Preston. Hell, it's his daughter."

"That's smart, and it should cover our asses too."

"All right, put Joe back on."

Preston took the phone from Drake and looked at it a second before placing it to his ear.

"Yes, Hank?"

"If you don't come back here with Cindy, don't come back at all. And remember, Billy is your responsibility. Don't fuck this up, Joe. If you do, you'll not only be out of a job and homeless, but I might ask the law to look into what happened to your wife. You get me?"

"I understand. Goodbye, Hank."

Drake stared down at Preston. "We're doing this, right?"

"Yeah, let's go."

They piled out of the room, gathered the rest of their men, and headed their caravan of rented trucks down the highway. And as they drove along, Preston vomited out the window.

34
THE TRUTH

SARA TENSED UP AS A CAR CAME TO A HARD STOP BEHIND her, but when she saw Garner at the wheel, she relaxed.

The handsome FBI agent left his vehicle and slid into Sara's passenger seat.

She smiled at him. "Thank you for sticking with me."

Garner pointed across the road at Rossetti's house.

"I can still walk over there and warn Rossetti that this whole thing is a set up, and I will if you don't tell me the truth."

"What are you talking about?"

"I talked to Marty Brewer. He told me you passed up a spot on the Terrorism Task Force last year so you could stay on Tanner's trail. Most agents would kill to get on that team rather than chase some two-bit hit man."

Sara gave a sarcastic laugh. "Two-bit hit man? You really have no idea who you're after, do you?"

"I'll admit it, he's left quite a trail behind him today as far as body count goes, but every one of those men was out to kill him, or so he thought. That would make it self-defense."

"What about the pimp yesterday? He murdered him and the others for their money and vehicle."

"There's no proof that was Tanner, although it likely was."

"It was him. He chose to go up against three armed men rather than rob a store for money. It's because he has no fear. And the bastard always wins, no matter the odds, that son of a bitch just keeps coming out on top."

"He's been extremely lucky, but it will run out someday."

Sara's gaze turned hot and her face flushed with anger as she stabbed a finger at Garner.

"You've read the reports, the intelligence gathered; you can't possibly believe he's not who he claims to be. Luck can't explain the things he's done."

Garner cast a cynical look her way as he realized what she was asking.

"The legend of Tanner? That myth has been around for about a hundred years. This Tanner is not the latest in a long line of elite assassins, Sara. He's just another hit man."

"I'll admit that much of it is supposition, but it's a mountain of supposition. Maybe advance training explains what makes him so good, and so hard to kill."

"He's exceptionally hard to kill, and he's smart; I'll grant you that. Despite what we suspect about him, he's never left a print behind at a murder site, including today. Hell, he'd never even been arrested until the Mexicans caught him with those drugs. Even now, no one knows his name. All we know is that he calls himself Tanner."

"Bullshit legend or not, he's killed dozens over the years, and goddamn it, Tanner killed Brian. He killed my… my CI."

Garner watched with sympathy as tears rolled down Sara's cheeks.

He reached over and took her hand. "Brian Ames wasn't just your CI, was he? He was your lover, and I'm guessing that you loved him very much."

Sara squeezed her eyes shut in a vain attempt to hold back the tears. Seeing the pain etched on her face, Garner knew he had guessed the truth.

He gave her hand a gentle squeeze before letting it go, then passed over the box of tissues that were sitting in the car's center console.

"We'll get Tanner, Sara. We'll sit back and let this war happen and then we'll use it to hang Tanner with, and he'll spend the rest of his life rotting behind bars."

Sara had composed herself. She looked over at Garner with eyes that were red from crying.

"Three meals a day in a comfy cell, do you think that's justice?"

Garner sighed. "I think it's all we've got and that it's not our job to play judge and jury."

Sara said nothing more. She didn't give a damn about acting as judge and jury. In her eyes, Tanner was guilty. He had killed the man she loved. It was time to carry out the sentence, and the sentence was death.

She would not act as judge and jury; she would be his executioner.

35
HOOKERS AND BLOW

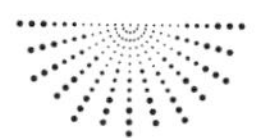

MERLE AND EARL CARTER STOOD GUARD OUTSIDE Rossetti's home while praying that O'Grady's men wouldn't attack.

Ramone had armed them with sawed-off shotguns, which would do them little good if even one of O'Grady's men had a rifle with a scope.

Merle felt like a sacrificial lamb and figured they were only given the shotguns because the weapons were loud, and if fired, would warn those within the house; the house that provided cover.

"Earl."

"Yeah?"

"Whatever you do, don't fire first. Hell, don't even raise the gun. Just keep it pointed at the ground, then maybe no one will shoot at us."

"We have to get out of here, Merle. Grabbin' Tanner was one thing, but fightin' a war is another. And tell me somethin', are we even gettin' paid for this?"

Merle shrugged. "Rossetti let us live after we lost Tanner; maybe he figures that's payment enough."

"Damn Tanner! We should have shot him when we had the chance."

"Maybe it's a good thing we didn't."

Earl turned and stared at his brother. "What the hell are you talkin' about? If we had shot him instead of usin' the stun gun, we'd be ten grand richer and Rossetti would have drowned us in hookers and blow."

"I heard a few of the guys talkin' in there. It sounds like the Conglomerate isn't too happy with Tanner anymore. They say if he makes this hit on Rossetti, that they'll hit him."

"So? What's that mean to us?"

"It's just a rumor, but they're sayin' the contract will be for fifty grand, and I don't know about you, but if I'm gonna whack Tanner, I'd rather do it for fifty G's than ten."

"Holy shit, fifty grand?"

"That's what they say. Maybe it's all bullshit, and anyway, Rossetti's still alive."

At the top of the hill past the winding driveway, a pickup truck slowed to a stop out on the roadway.

A few seconds passed before the driver stepped out and raised a pair of binoculars to his eyes. The man was tall, had an angular build, and wore jeans along with a flannel shirt that was too warm for the weather.

Merle cursed. "I think that's one of O'Grady's men, the dude looks like he's checkin' the place out."

The man lowered the binoculars and let them hang from a strap around his neck, then took out a cell phone to make a call. A minute passed, then three more pickup trucks parked behind the first one.

"Earl."

"Yeah?"

"When nobody's lookin', we run."

"Hell yeah," Earl said, and once more wished that he had killed Tanner when he had the chance.

36

TEN IS MORE THAN SIX

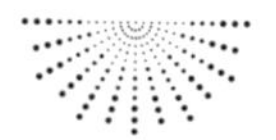

O'GRADY'S MAN, DRAKE, TOOK THE BINOCULARS FROM the man in the flannel shirt and trained them on the cars parked at the side of Rossetti's house.

"Preston!"

Cindy's father got out of one of the pickup trucks and walked over to stand by Drake.

"What is it?"

"I thought you said that Rossetti had only six guys guarding him?"

"That's what Buck told me."

"Buck is a bartender and a wannabe actor, not a soldier. Hell, I see at least ten cars down there, and ten is more than six. Plus, you can be damn sure they didn't all drive here alone."

"That device Hank gave us says that Cindy's phone is in there, which means she's in there. We can't go back without her, or we'll all be out of a job."

Drake spat at the ground. He was an ex-soldier, had fought in Iraq, been wounded, and barely survived. He was no coward, but he wasn't looking to get killed in Vegas.

What happens in Vegas might stay in Vegas, but not his ass, not six feet under.

"Let's get back in the trucks. I want to think this over."

SARA WATCHED O'GRADY'S MEN THROUGH HER OWN SET OF binoculars.

"They've climbed back in their trucks and now they're just sitting there."

"Maybe they've come to their senses," Garner said, then he looked around. "Hey, if Tanner is waiting for the fireworks to begin, then where is he?"

Sara lowered the binoculars. "He's here somewhere, or he soon will be."

"Maybe he's coming from the rear, but no, there's nothing past that ridge but scrubland."

"He doesn't need to be close enough to see anything. He just has to be near enough to hear. If they start fighting they'll make a racket, especially those two at the front door with the shotguns."

"So, you think he'll make a frontal assault?"

Sara made a face. "I have no idea what Tanner might do, but he's coming, you can be sure he's coming."

TANNER WAS FOUR HUNDRED YARDS AWAY, BUMPING ALONG in the motor home across desert scrubland that damn near bogged down the tires. The engine was running hot, which told Tanner he was losing oil, but he only needed to drive for a few more seconds and he'd be in position.

He remembered the exterior layout of Rossetti's home from having scouted it weeks ago before going to prison, and so he knew exactly where to position the motor home.

Before driving toward the house, Tanner had wiped down the RV for prints, although, he was certain that once the propane tank blew, that the fire would erase any DNA evidence. The owners had also stored several extra 20lb. canisters aboard.

He'd been watching O'Grady's men and had spied Merle and Earl at the front door, but as he had guessed, neither O'Grady's men nor Rossetti's thugs were eager to engage each other. That was all right, he'd give things a push.

He parked the motor home on a slope facing downward atop the sandy ridge that bordered Rossetti's home on three sides. He then vacated his seat, only to fill it with one of the mannequins he had taken from the clothing store in the mall.

The other dummy was already positioned in the passenger seat, and both mannequins wore hoodies pulled up, with sunglasses glued in place.

Up close they'd fool no one, but from a distance they'd look like men, and since he had replaced the RV's Nevada plates with the Colorado ones he'd taken off the white pickup, Rossetti was sure to figure that O'Grady had brought in more troops.

Tanner gathered the bags of ice he'd bought earlier and tossed them out the back window, then he climbed out, jammed the bags under the rear wheels, and poked holes in them so they would drain once melted.

After climbing back in and staying low, he released the parking brake and felt the motor home lurch forward.

Just when he thought he would have to engage the parking brake again, the vehicle stopped moving.

After opening the valve on the propane tank, Tanner

climbed out once again and saw that the ice was working as a wheel chock, as he had hoped. However, the ice was a temporary chock, one that would melt in the heat of the day and send the RV careening down the slope and into the side of Rossetti's home. Then, once the propane gas blew, the fire would begin.

The fat man would be driven from his home by not only gunfire, but also flames, and when he used his tunnel to escape, Tanner would be waiting. Waiting and ready to kill.

Tanner moved away from the vehicle, staying low and circling around to the rear of the house. His shotgun was at the ready, his heart was filled with murder.

37

ONE ROTTEN SNEAKY BASTARD

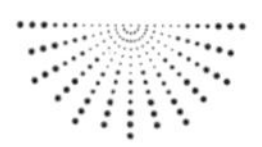

Ramone held the curtain aside in the dining room, as he pointed out the motor home to Rossetti.

Rossetti's eyebrows knitted together.

"How many guys are in that thing?"

"I don't know. You can see two shapes in the front there, but I can't make out much else because of the glare."

Up on the ridge, the ice bags drained water, causing the heavy vehicle to shift. Rossetti pointed at it.

"Did you see that? It just moved, like there's a lot of guys inside milling around. Let's not wait for them to come to us, let's go to them. Send those two idiot brothers to check it out."

Ramone smiled. "If there are as many guys up there as we think, those two will get perforated."

"I know, but with that FBI bitch keeping an eye on the place, we can't start anything. Let Tweedledee and Tweedledum act as bait, but make sure they know not to start shooting first."

"I'll make sure they know."

Drake dropped the binoculars and let them hang around his neck.

All he could see of the driver in the RV was a side view of a hooded head, due to the glare from the setting sun. He jogged back down the road a couple hundred feet, and that's when he saw that the vehicle had plates from his home state.

"Preston, did Hank say anything about sending more guys?"

"No, why?"

Drake ignored the question and rubbed a hand over his beard.

"What the hell is going on?"

From her viewpoint further down and across the road, Sara squinted into her binoculars.

"It's got Colorado plates, so it must be more of O'Grady's men."

"More men? He must not have anyone left on the ranch," Garner said.

Sara raised up the binoculars and focused on the driver. After adjusting the lens to make certain that what she was seeing was real, she laughed.

"Oh, Tanner, you are one rotten sneaky bastard."

"What are you looking at?"

Sara passed the binoculars to Garner and told him to take a good look at the driver.

After a few seconds, Garner lowered them as his mouth dropped open.

"Mannequins?"

"That's right. He's diverting everyone's attention. Rossetti is probably thinking he's outnumbered and the Colorado bunch must be wondering who the new guys are."

Sara opened her door and walked around to the trunk.

"It's time to put on the vests and get ready to move. Tanner is here."

38

OH, NOW I GET IT

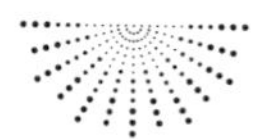

MERLE POINTED UP AT THE MOTOR HOME. "YOU WANT US to go up there?"

Ramone nodded to him. He had walked Merle and Earl to the side of the home and explained what Rossetti wanted them to do.

"Like I said, just go over and take a look. Try to figure out how many guys are on board and what weapons they have."

Earl tugged at his collar. "What if they shoot at us?"

"I suggest you duck," Ramone said.

"You want us to go now?" Merle asked.

"Wait five minutes. If they don't make a move, you go up there and see what you can see."

"Are we getting paid for this?" Earl said.

"Of course, and when it's over, you'll get your money."

"If we're still alive," Merle said.

"I could have Vinny place you back in the basement if that's what you want."

Merle swallowed hard. "No sir, we'll do what you say."

"Good, I knew we could count on you."

RAMONE WENT BACK INSIDE AND WAS HEADED TOWARD THE office when an idea occurred to him. He stopped in the foyer and took out the phone that Tanner had given him.

He had never even mentioned the phone to Rossetti, because he knew there was no way the man would agree to pay a million dollars in extortion.

Ramone thought this dispute with O'Grady was stupid, and he was not looking forward to dying in a battle that would gain them nothing. What the hell was there for them to take from O'Grady, cattle? This whole mess was just O'Grady and Rossetti trying to see whose dick was bigger.

As Tanner had said, there was only one number in the phone's address book. Ramone heard it ring five times before a gruff voice answered.

"Cindy? Where are you?"

"This uh, this isn't Cindy. My name is Ramone and I'm trying to reach Hank O'Grady."

"Ramone? You sound different."

"O'Grady? I don't know what you're talking about, but we've never spoken to each other before. The only one of your people I ever talked to was Joe Preston."

There was silence on the line, but then O'Grady spoke. "Describe Preston to me."

"White guy, about thirty, kind of handsome, full head of hair."

"Joe Preston is in his forties with a bald spot, and he isn't handsome."

"What is going on here?" Ramone said, more to himself than to O'Grady.

"Listen here, Ramone, or whoever you are, Joe Preston, the real Joe Preston met with a guy named

Ramone and gave him fifty thousand dollars to get back his daughter, Cindy."

"I never heard of a Cindy, but I gave a guy named Joe Preston fifty grand when we met at the mall here. He was with a man named Tanner."

"I've never heard of anyone named Tanner, but Preston handed someone named Ramone money at a mall in Vegas. What the hell is going on out there?"

Ramone waved his left arm in a wide gesture, as if to disburse the confusion.

"Just tell me one thing, O'Grady. Do you have a beef with Al Rossetti?"

"I do if he's holding Cindy hostage."

"I told you, we don't know anything about a Cindy."

"You're using her phone right now; her name came up on the caller ID, and my men tracked her to that location by tracing her phone."

"Tanner gave me this phone."

"Tanner? Who's this Tanner you keep talking about? One of your guys?"

"No, but I think he's behind everything. Listen, O'Grady, call your guys and tell them to stand down. I think you and Rossetti need to talk."

"First, I'll talk to Rossetti, and then we'll see."

"Fair enough, hold on, I have to go find him."

Ramone rushed through the house, while silently cursing Tanner every step of the way.

39
DUCK AND COVER

"THEY'RE DUMMIES," EARL SAID, AS HE AND HIS BROTHER stood twenty feet in front of the RV.

Merle cocked his head. "Maybe it's run by remote control, like those cars we stole when we was kids."

Earl wrinkled his nose. "You smell that?"

Merle sniffed the air "Yeah, it smells like rotten eggs."

"Nah, I know that smell, that's propane."

"Somebody must be having a cookout."

"Probably Rossetti, you know that fat fuck can throw down some food."

Merle laughed. "Don't let him hear you say that."

"So, what should we do, look inside?"

"I guess," Merle said and took a step forward.

RAMONE WAS HALFWAY BACK TO THE OFFICE WHEN HE remembered the orders he'd given Merle and Earl. He turned around, but then stopped as a revelation struck him.

Merle and Earl were the ones who first mentioned O'Grady, and they said that O'Grady's men snatched Tanner from them, but O'Grady never heard of Tanner.

Those bastards are working for Tanner.

Ramone cursed under his breath and ran back outside, where he found Merle and Earl approaching the motor home.

"Hey! Get back here."

The brothers turned at the sound of Ramone's voice, but then whipped back around. The motor home had lurched forward and was rolling toward them, because more water had leaked from the bags of ice beneath the rear wheels.

The brothers gave each other a stricken look, then dropped to the ground. The huge vehicle rumbled over them and identical bolts fastened on both sides of the undercarriage caught their collars and ripped the shirts right off them. The hard tug also jerked their heads up and they received solid whacks to the back of their skulls.

After the RV passed, Merle and Earl rolled over, sat up looking dazed, and watched the vehicle pick up speed as it headed for the house.

Ramone saw the motor home roll over the Carter brothers and figured they were dead. He also realized he had been too late to stop the war, and now the only thing to do was to win it.

He whipped his gun off his hip, flipped off the safety, and took aim at the driver, whose hood had fallen back from its face.

In the same instant Ramone realized the driver was a mannequin, he had applied pressure to his weapon's trigger, which sent a bullet into the RV, ignited a spark, and blew him to hell.

40
THE MISSIONARY POSITION

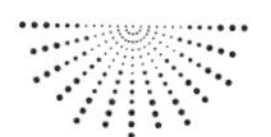

SARA SHUT HER EYES TIGHT AGAINST THE STINGING SAND AS the blast of the motor home spread debris over a wide area.

In the next instant, she was slammed to the ground, hitting her head and becoming rattled, but when she opened her eyes and focused, Garner was lying atop her like a lover.

"What the hell, Jake?"

Garner sighed with relief, rolled off Sara, then pointed back toward where she'd been standing. That's when Sara saw that a large chunk of the motor home's roof was sizzling in that very spot and had landed in the car's trunk.

"Oh my God, you saved me."

"What are partners for?" Garner said, as he helped her up from the ground, before taking out his cell. "I'll call this in."

Sara galloped toward the house. "I'll get Tanner."

Garner shouted, "Sara, wait!" but she was already gone.

At the house, four pickup trucks came to a stop and Drake and the rest of O'Grady's men piled out.

Drake pointed at the front doors, which Ramone had left open in his haste to reach Merle and Earl.

"The doors are wide open. Let's go show these Vegas punks that they messed with the wrong guys."

The men shouted and followed Drake inside, all but one that is. Cindy's father, Joe Preston, looked down at the device in his hand and saw that Cindy's phone no longer registered as coming from inside the house, but rather, from across the road.

Preston climbed back into the last of the trucks, which still had the key in the ignition. He turned it around and drove out toward the road as the sounds of a firefight raged behind him, and smoke billowed into the sky.

When he reached the top of the driveway, he slammed on the brakes. He had nearly run Sara down as she rushed toward the house. They exchanged brief glances, then Preston drove across the road and into a field of scrub brush.

He found the phone almost immediately, where it had landed in the sand. When he saw the streak of blood on it, he felt his world slipping away. This feeling wasn't caused by the possible loss of his daughter, but rather by the fear of losing his job.

Preston rode away from the house, away from his comrades, while racking his brain over what to do next.

Tanner had made it around to the rear of the house but was hidden from view behind the ridge. When the motor home blew, he was surprised by the force of the explosion, but knew that after viewing the carnage, Rossetti would be heading for his tunnel.

Tanner was outside the tunnel's exit, where Dwight Sorrell had said it would be, inside a decrepit wooden shack with a missing door. The shack sat yards away from an old stone well and there was an ATV parked nearby, an All-Terrain Vehicle. That told Tanner that Rossetti had planned to flee all along.

Inside the house, something boomed loudly. Tanner listened and heard several different weapons firing at once, as outside smoke rose skyward from the fire at the side of the home.

After tossing the Mossberg atop the roof of the shack, Tanner pulled himself up onto the structure. When he stood, he could just see over the bunkhouse and pool to the rear of the home.

The sun was setting, and night was on its way.

Tanner lay flat atop the roof, grabbed the shotgun, and waited for Rossetti to exit the tunnel. Night was coming, but for Rossetti, there would be no dawn.

41
INEVITABLE

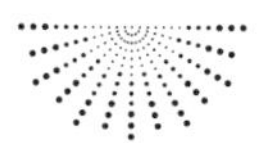

INSIDE HIS OFFICE, ROSSETTI SHOUTED IN FRUSTRATION AS Ramone failed to answer his phone.

Ramone had the damn key to the ATV they were to escape in, but then Rossetti remembered the spare key inside the shack. He relaxed and headed for the closet door.

He had no idea what had caused the explosion that had rocked the house, but he figured that Tanner was behind it.

Rossetti ripped open the closet and gasped at Joy's body. He'd forgotten he had stuck her there. He decided he would hide the corpse in the tunnel as he made his escape.

He hit the hidden latch beneath a shelf and pushed against the back wall, which caused the surface to swing outward on spring hinges.

Rossetti felt the coolness of the passage as he gazed into the dark, and thanked God that an old-time thug named Frankie the Fish had built the tunnel.

There was a switch inside. Rossetti pushed it upwards and turned on the string of incandescent bulbs strung along the top of the passage's left wall. He then reached back, grabbed Joy by the ankles, and dragged her body inside.

After shutting the door, he checked to see if any light showed around its edges. He saw none, assumed it was sealed tight, then shuffled his corpulent form down the tunnel's slanting floor. His footsteps echoed off the concrete walls as he descended beneath the earth.

The tunnel curved twice, the first time as it neared the area of the swimming pool, and a second time to move its trajectory back toward the shack, after passing beneath the bunkhouse. The shack sat atop a small hill. Once Rossetti reached the other end, he had to climb up a ladder.

At the foot of the ladder, Rossetti made a sound of disgust as he realized he had to holster his gun to climb. The act rendered him defenseless. If Tanner showed up while he was on the ladder, Rossetti knew he'd be a dead man.

As he neared the top, he grinned. Tanner had no way of knowing about the tunnel, so Rossetti figured he would soon be out of Tanner's reach. There was an ATV outside the shack, and a short drive north through the desert would place him at an airfield, where a plane was waiting.

He'd be in Reno in no time, safe from Tanner and O'Grady. Once he was settled there, he would plan his revenge against both men.

When he was four rungs from the top, he was nearly in total blackness, but knew that the trapdoor was above him. The door was a three-foot square of pine planking and opened on hinges. An old throw rug covered it, with a wooden table positioned above it.

After sliding a bolt and unlocking the trapdoor, Rossetti pushed, saw pale daylight through a gap, and turned his head about looking for feet and other signs of an ambush.

He saw nothing suspicious, but when he pushed harder, the door refused to flip up.

It was the table he realized, one of its legs must be sitting atop the door. Rossetti let the door fall back in place, raised up both hands, and shoved with all his strength. After the table toppled over onto its side, Rossetti lifted the door and it hung open, kept from falling over by a chain.

The big man clambered up into the small room in clumsy fashion, making it first to his knees and then his feet. He was sweating from the short walk and climb, but he breathed a sigh of relief as he removed his gun and looked about.

On one wall were several wooden shelves that held ancient nails and hammers, while in a corner, there leaned nearly a dozen old pickaxes and shovels.

He checked the floor, which was perpetually coated with sand blown in from outside. There were no shoe prints in the sand, but there was half of one near the door. Rossetti guessed that Ramone had made it when he reached in to hang the spare ATV key on a nail.

Rossetti plucked the key from the wall. After poking his head out and looking both ways, he strode outside with a smile on his lips and made a beeline for the ATV.

Tanner heard wood scraping, followed by a crash, as Rossetti flipped up the trapdoor in the shack and toppled an old table.

Tanner kept himself flat atop the tar papered roof and waited for Rossetti to show himself, while wondering how many men would be with him.

Not knowing that Ramone had died in the blast, Tanner was surprised to see Rossetti exit the shack alone, but gratified at last to be on the verge of fulfilling his contract.

Tanner had glanced behind him just seconds ago and verified that no one else was nearby, so he stood, called Rossetti's name, and watched the rotund hoodlum stop and turn.

Rossetti's eyes were darting about in fear, his gun ready, then finding Tanner perched atop the roof, his eyes grew wide with wonder and he raised his hand to fire.

Tanner blasted Rossetti with the shotgun and Rossetti's weapon flew away, along with the fingers on his right hand.

Rossetti squirmed in the dirt while wailing in agony, that was followed by a yelp of terror, as Tanner jumped to the ground.

"Tanner… listen, we can… we can still come to an, an understanding, you, ya know?"

Tanner simply shook his head.

Rossetti looked around for help, but he was alone. When he gazed back up at Tanner, there was a look of acceptance in his eyes.

Tanner placed the shotgun against Rossetti's chest.

"It was inevitable."

The shotgun boomed, Rossetti died, and the contract was fulfilled.

42
YOU NEVER KNOW WHEN YOU'LL NEED AN UMBRELLA

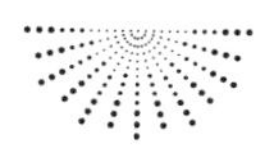

After insuring that help was on the way in the form of more agents, along with fire and medical personnel, Garner had sprinted toward the burning house.

When Tanner fired the shot that shredded Rossetti's hand, Garner had spotted the muzzle flash through the swirl of smoke and wondered why it had appeared above ground level and far from the house.

That was when he remembered the binoculars were hanging around his neck. He raised them up and saw Tanner's back from the waist up, just visible above the roof of the bunkhouse.

"Shit!"

Garner tried calling Sara, but she wasn't answering her phone, and he prayed that she was all right.

As he rounded the side of the bunkhouse, he heard the second blast, and moved up the hill in silence.

SARA STEPPED OVER YET ANOTHER DEAD RANCH HAND AND fired at the man who was responsible for the body, a young punk with a mullet and enough gold chains to open a pawnshop.

The punk fell to the floor, blood spurting from a wound in his thigh like the bullet had struck oil. Sara realized the slug had hit him in the femoral artery. The man began screaming in agony, and as she drew nearer, he begged Sara for help.

She kicked his gun out of reach and continued toward Rossetti's office, knowing the punk would bleed out in minutes.

She didn't care. She didn't care who lived or who died. Her only concern was to find Tanner and end him.

She was carrying an assault rifle, a Heckler & Koch MP5, along with her everyday weapon, a Glock 21 SF, which she used to blow apart the lock on Rossetti's office door.

She entered low, and after verifying the main room was empty, she shut the office door as best she could, then propped a chair beneath the doorknob. The smoke from the fire hadn't traveled far back into the home yet, where the office was, and she wanted to keep it out for as long as possible, while also making it difficult to enter.

The bathroom was empty, and Sara could see into the closet, but there was blood on the floor near the desk and splattered on the wall beside it. Sara feared that Tanner had killed Rossetti and moved on. However, no sooner did she have the thought she dismissed it.

It would take more than one man to move Rossetti's corpse, and why would Tanner even bother. She gave the stain a closer look and realized that it was already drying. Whoever had been hurt, had been injured before the fighting began.

The blood trailed off in a thin, intermittent streak that led into the closet. Sara approached it with caution, although there appeared to be no room to hide.

Nothing, just office supplies, umbrellas, and an overcoat.

She was about to search elsewhere when she spotted more blood in a corner and noticed strands of red hair sticking out from the bottom of the back wall.

What the hell?

She pressed her left hand against the wall and felt it give just a bit. "Is someone in there?"

With no answer, she plucked one of the umbrellas from its stand and used the metal tip of it to poke a hole in the wall. When the hole was big enough, she looked through with one eye and saw a row of lights dangling along a concrete wall, while a look downward revealed a pair of shapely legs.

"Hello? Hey! Wake up! Can you hear me?"

There was no answer again. Sara tore at the wall savagely, first with the umbrella, and then with the base of a heavy floor lamp taken from the office.

When the aperture was large enough, Sara squeezed through, then cursed as she saw Joy's battered corpse.

"Rossetti, you son of a bitch," she mumbled. Then she heard the faint, echoing sound of a shotgun blast, followed by barely audible wails of pain. "Tanner?"

Sara dashed along the tunnel headed for Tanner while aching for revenge, as her heart grew cold as a stone.

43
SHE DID WARN HIM

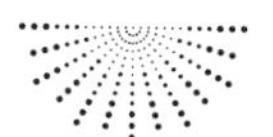

TANNER WAS TURNING FROM ROSSETTI'S CORPSE WHEN HE saw something glinting near the body.

It was a key reflecting in the last rays of daylight, and Tanner realized it was meant for Rossetti's getaway vehicle, the ATV.

He bent over to retrieve it, and as his fingers gripped it a voice boomed behind him, the voice of Special Agent Jake Garner.

"FBI! Drop your weapon and place your hands over your head."

Tanner straightened slowly, while still holding the Mossberg in one hand and palming the ignition key in the other. His hands were gloved, as they always were when making a hit.

"I said, drop it!"

Tanner weighed his options and decided it was best to appear cooperative, a posture that might lure the lawman closer while it was still just the two of them. He tossed the shotgun atop Rossetti's body and raised his hands.

Tanner was expecting to hear Garner tell him to get on

the ground. Instead, he watched as Garner tossed a set of handcuffs toward him, to land at his feet.

"Put one end on your wrist and then attach the other end to the well."

Tanner turned his head and stared at the well.

It was made of stone at its base, but there was rusted metal embedded into it and sitting over the hole like a trellis.

He figured it was likely the part that once held a rope and bucket. Once he was secured to it, he could kiss his freedom goodbye.

Garner took a step closer and aimed his gun at Tanner's face. "Do it or die, your choice."

Tanner stared into Garner's eyes and saw that the man was serious. Always the pragmatist, Tanner bent over and picked up the cuffs. "Whatever you say, Officer."

Scrambling sounds came from the shack, causing Garner to jerk his head around to look inside.

Seeing his chance, Tanner rushed forward only to freeze as Garner spun back around and jammed the barrel of the gun against Tanner's stomach.

"Back up!"

Tanner did so with a sigh, then watched as a dark-haired woman exited the shack, with FBI credentials hanging from a chain around her neck.

Tanner knew he had seen her beautiful face before, but he couldn't recall the context in which he'd last seen it. When he searched her eyes, he was surprised by the intense glare of hatred burning within them.

Garner stared at Sara with a confused look on his face. "Were you in that shack all this time?"

Sara answered him while glowering at Tanner.

"There's a tunnel that leads to Rossetti's office."

"Oh, well, as you can see, I have a gift for you."

"Take a walk, Jake. Tanner is mine."

"Calm down, Sara. We have him. We've caught him. Don't endanger your career for this piece of shit."

Sara took her eyes off Tanner as she spoke to her partner.

"Leave, Garner. Leave and don't look back."

Garner turned his head to look at her and Tanner moved right, closer to the ATV. Sara caught the movement and raised her gun.

Garner pushed her arm down with one hand while shouting at Tanner.

"Goddamn it, Tanner. Get down on the ground now or I swear we'll both shoot you."

Tanner was near enough to the ATV to touch it, but knew he'd be shot if he moved any closer.

He got down on his knees, stared at Sara, and asked a question.

"Who are you?"

"Special Agent Blake, I'm Sara Blake."

"Why do you hate me?"

"Because you killed Brian. Brian Ames."

Tanner recalled the name and remembered why Sara looked familiar. She had been Ames's lover. He had seen them together as he followed Ames and learned his routine.

Ames had been an accountant and money washer for the New York branch of the Conglomerate, but he had turned snitch.

Tanner had killed him, painless and quick, while Ames sat waiting at a table at an outdoor cafe in New York City. He had fired a single shot behind Ames's right ear with a silenced gun.

The bullet was of low caliber and, after entering

Ames's skull, it ricocheted inside his head, lacking the force to cause an exit wound.

The slug shredded Brian Ames's brain, causing his death, while the slight noise of the shot was swallowed up by the sounds of the city street.

The fact that he had been hit in daylight in the middle of Manhattan was to ensure that Ames's death would be newsworthy, to discourage anyone else in the Conglomerate who might be thinking of talking.

Frank Richards had ordered that hit as well, along with the instructions to make it public.

Tanner cocked his head as understanding dawned. "You were the one Ames was waiting for that day, weren't you?"

"I found him, you son of a bitch. I walked up to the table and—" Sara paused, while attempting to compose herself, even as tears ran down her cheeks. When she spoke again, her voice was at a higher pitch and forced through a throat grown tight with emotion.

"His eyes were open, open and staring, and I remember smiling and thinking that he was daydreaming, but… when I leaned over and kissed him… oh God, his lips, his lips were already cold."

Tanner said nothing, because there was nothing to say. If he told her he was sorry, it would be a lie. He was not sorry. Killing Brian Ames was a bit of business to him, nothing more and nothing less. As a grown man, Ames surely knew if his superiors discovered his betrayal that he would be dealt with in the manner he was.

Tanner gazed at Sara. Behind the hatred and the pain, he glimpsed something else, guilt. The woman felt guilty, and he knew then that it was Sara who had turned Ames and got him to talk.

Sara took a deep breath, wiped at her eyes, and raised her gun once more.

"No!" Garner said.

"Leave, Garner. Leave me alone with this man and let me do what I came here to do."

Garner placed a hand on her arm again. "Sara, I won't let you do this."

"Goddamn it! I said leave. Don't make me tell you again."

Garner moved in front of her, blocking her shot.

Sara lowered her head and glared at him through hooded eyes.

"Get the fuck out of my way."

"No partner, I'm not going to let you—"

The first two bullets caught Garner in the vest, just as Sara intended, but as he reacted and turned away, the third bullet cut through a seam and blood flowed from the wound in his side.

Garner fell to the dirt, his gun slipping from his hand, and Sara kicked it aside, as her eyes flicked between Garner and Tanner.

Garner raised a hand, said "Why?" in a weak voice, then his eyes closed, and he stopped moving.

Sara winced at the sight of Garner's bloody wound, but when she locked her eyes on Tanner, she smiled.

"He's my partner and I kind of like him, so you can just imagine what I'm going to do to you."

44
FAT PEOPLE ARE HANDY TO HAVE AROUND

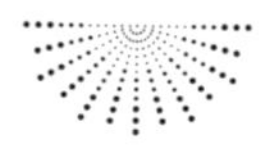

SARA STARED AT TANNER ACROSS THE BODY OF HIS LATEST target, Albert Rossetti and that of her partner, Jake Garner.

Rossetti was Tanner's handiwork, but Garner lay dying because of Sara.

"You don't feel any regret at all over murdering Brian, do you?" Sara asked.

"No."

"What was Brian's life worth to you? What did they pay you?"

"I charged ten thousand, had he been aware that he was targeted and gone into hiding, I would have charged much more."

"I should have placed him under protection, but we were certain no one knew he was willing to talk."

"I was told they had cameras in his apartment, in the bedroom," Tanner said.

It was a lie, but he hoped that the thought of being filmed unknowingly while making love would distract her. And while they talked, Tanner oh so slowly shifted his weight, taking pressure off his knees and transferring it to the balls of his feet, as he prepared to leap at Sara.

"Video? They filmed us?"

"Yes, but I never saw it. I only needed a photo of Ames."

Sara appeared stricken and her face scrunched up as if she were about to cry, but then she emitted a low chuckle, as she smiled at Tanner.

"Nice try, Tanner, and come on, leap at me. Maybe you'll make it before I put one in your face."

Tanner scowled at her. She had been toying with him. He had thought himself seconds away from being shot to death, but her smile made him wonder if she was planning to take him somewhere to be tortured.

"What's your next move?" Tanner asked, as the sound of sirens carried on the wind.

"We're going to stay here until I'm certain my partner gets medical attention. After that, I'll arrest you and take you away."

"Never to be seen again," Tanner said, and Sara nodded.

"Fasten those cuffs behind your back. Refuse and I'll fire a shot into your shoulder."

Tanner gazed around, searching for a way out and finding none. To the south, near the front of the home, was a red haze above which smoke billowed into an ever-darkening sky.

Tanner placed one end of the cuffs around his left wrist and clamped it shut, locking it in place.

As he was about to secure the other end, two figures emerged from around the side of the shack.

It was Merle and Earl.

They were naked from the waist up after having their shirts ripped away by the undercarriage of the RV. Their skin was reddened from the heat of the blast, and mottled with sand from lying on the ground.

Their eyelashes were gone, seared away from having been so close to the heat of the fire, and their hair was also singed, the end of each strand blackened and curled.

They still had the shotguns, but they carried them loosely by their barrels and pointed skyward. Their eyes were unfocused.

The rear of their skulls had slammed against the bottom of the motor home, leaving both men to travel about dazed and moving aimlessly in what was an intensified version of their normal state.

In the dusky light of a fading day, Sara saw the shotguns before registering any other details. She barked out an order to the brothers to drop their weapons. They stopped walking, looked startled, and the weapons fell to the dirt.

Sara had taken her eyes off Tanner for only a moment and assumed that he would use that flash of time to attempt escape by means of the ATV, or perhaps come charging at her.

She fired even as she turned, and her shot ricocheted off the side of the ATV, with Tanner nowhere in sight.

Sara stared, looking at the land beyond the vehicle, searching for Tanner, then she caught movement on her peripheral, to the left. It was Tanner.

He had dived beside Rossetti's massive corpse and was using it as a shield to hide behind. Sara turned just in time to see a hand snake out and grab the Mossberg that laid atop the body.

She dove to the ground as the Mossberg boomed.

TANNER GREETED THE APPEARANCE OF THE CARTER brothers with a smile and launched himself to twist in midair and land on his back beside Rossetti's body, which had three times his thickness and would act as temporary cover.

He reached up with his right hand and snatched back the shotgun he had tossed away earlier, then fired high.

Killing the female FBI agent would be ideal in the short run, but the consequences of killing a federal agent would be unending and make him a priority target for the law.

He didn't need that kind of heat, so he fired high, jacked another shell, and waited for return fire, knowing that it would give Sara's position away.

He felt Rossetti's corpse vibrate from the impact of the round before he registered the shot.

She was to the right of him, taking cover behind the front of the ATV.

Tanner sprang up and fired, once again spraying buckshot over Sara's head. Afterward, he ran toward the shack and dived low, covering the last ten feet with a leap amid gunfire, and slammed into the floor of the shack just inches from the entrance to the tunnel.

SARA CURSED AS SHE WATCHED TANNER PROPEL HIMSELF into the shack and realized her shots had missed him.

Tanner was headed for the tunnel. If he made it into the house, he might disappear in all the chaos caused by the fire and gun battle.

The sound of sirens was loud and stationary, and red and blue lights flickered at the front of the home.

Sara blinked in surprise when she saw that the Carter

brothers hadn't moved since dropping their weapons, and they watched her run toward the shack with dazed, dull eyes, like cattle watching a farmer plow a field.

After crouching low and peeking around the doorframe, Sara entered the shack and headed for the entrance to the tunnel.

When she reached the bottom of the ladder, she paused, set the selector switch on the MP5 to full auto, and moved along the tunnel.

Her eyes were trained on the section ahead where the tunnel curved. She was ready for an ambush, while prepared to slaughter.

45
IT'S BEEN A HELL OF A DAY

TANNER WAITED SEVERAL SECONDS AFTER SARA CLIMBED down into the tunnel, before rising from concealment behind the overturned table, where he had curled himself into a tight ball.

He retrieved his shotgun from where he had propped it in the corner among the pickaxes and shovels, then went back outside.

Merle and Earl were still standing there, and Tanner spoke to them.

"It's been a hell of a day, hmm boys?"

They said nothing back, but just stood there, weaving.

Tanner ignored them and went to Garner. The Fed was still breathing, but he had lost blood and lay in a puddle of it. Tanner checked the agent's pockets and found the handcuff key. After using it to free the cuff on his wrist, he dialed Garner's phone.

When the 9-1-1 operator answered, Tanner said, "Officer down, near a shack at the rear of Al Rossetti's property." As the operator asked a question, Tanner dropped the phone atop Garner's still form.

Moments later, the ATV was in motion and headed toward the distant lights of the airfield.

SARA CURSED WITH WILD ABANDON AS SHE KICKED THE chair that she had earlier wedged against Rossetti's office door.

Tanner had tricked her somehow.

If he had gone through the tunnel, there would have been no way for him to leave the office without first moving that chair or unlocking the window, and she could see from where she stood that the window latch was secured.

She coughed, as smoke entered her lungs. The fire was still burning, although she could hear the rush of spraying water being used by the fire department.

Tanner, she had to find Tanner.

She rushed back to the closet, stepped over Joy's body, and traversed the tunnel passage once again. When she emerged, she found a pair of paramedics working on Garner. They had removed his vest and cut his shirt away to tend to the wound in his side.

Sara looked about, but saw neither Tanner nor the Carter brothers, then she realized that the ATV was gone as well. She gazed north and could see the lights of a vehicle in the desert, moving away.

Sara hung her head, then spoke to the paramedics. They were a man and a woman, both middle aged and both black.

"Will he live?"

The woman answered. "We think so, but he may have a collapsed lung, and he's lost a lot of blood."

Sara turned and ran toward the road. She needed a car

to get to the airfield. If she couldn't stop Tanner from flying off, she could at least have the Bureau track his flight.

The front of the house was a scene of pandemonium, where several more paramedics worked on wounded men, and the fire continued to burn not only the house, but it had also ignited a pair of parked cars.

Firefighters were spraying down the cars and the home. Their hoses and equipment made Sara's trip back to the road a circuitous one, as she navigated around fire equipment, ambulances, and chunks of debris.

The road was closed off to civilian traffic. Sara was about to commandeer a police car when she heard a glorious sound. It was a helicopter, and it was landing in a nearby field.

She rushed toward it, reaching it just after it put down, and filled her fellow agents in on Tanner's escape.

The helicopter rose into the night sky once more and went in pursuit. It took only seconds for the lights of the airfield to come into view, and Sara laughed with glee when she saw that the ATV was still a hundred yards shy of reaching it.

The pilot landed near the airfield, as the ATV came to a stop a short distance in front of its nose. The pilot, who was also an agent, spoke over the aircraft's loudspeaker.

"DRIVER! STEP OUT OF THE VEHICLE WITH YOUR HANDS HELD HIGH AND YOUR FINGERS SPREAD!"

THE INSTANT THE FIGURE EMERGED FROM THE ATV, SARA rushed forward with the MP5. She would have loved to torture Tanner, but she would settle for killing him outright.

"It's me, Tanner, Special Agent Blake."

She moved to her left to block the lights of the chopper, so that the glare wouldn't blind Tanner and he could see her face when she pulled the trigger.

The man stepped forward with his hands held high and Sara saw it was Merle Carter.

"No!"

She dropped her weapon, ran at Merle and tackled him to the sand.

"Where is he? Damn you! Where is Tanner?"

Merle shook his head and blinked, trying to focus on the words of the woman screaming at him.

"I don't know where he is, but I think he took my brother with him."

Sara moaned. Then she recalled the sight that greeted her when she emerged from the tunnel the second time.

Garner on his side, his vest removed, his shirt cut away, but there was no chain around his neck, the chain that held his FBI credentials.

Sara rolled over to lay atop her back in the sand, as sobs racked her body and despair filled her heart. She had risked everything, even the life of her partner, and all for nothing.

Tanner was gone.

46
SORRY ABOUT THAT WHOLE, YA KNOW, SHOOTING YOU THING

An APB was put out on both Earl and Tanner, but only Earl was located.

Tanner had left him inside Garner's car, handcuffed to the steering wheel, with Garner's credentials in the glove compartment.

Garner regained consciousness before going in for surgery, and Sara was held under house arrest in the Vegas field office until Garner could be questioned further.

When he did wake the following afternoon, he gave a full statement.

Sara said nothing. Refused to utter a single syllable, but when her boss, Martin Brewer, appeared in Vegas, she followed him into an interrogation room and confessed all.

After much back and forth between Brewer and other FBI officials, Sara was released, but told to stay in Vegas until further notice. She was also informed that if she left the city for any reason whatsoever, she would be labeled a fugitive, hunted down, and charged with the attempted murder of a federal officer.

~

Hank O'Grady placed the blame for everything on Cindy's father, Joe Preston.

O'Grady and his surviving men, of which there were only four, including Drake, testified that it was Preston who was behind the attack on Rossetti's home.

O'Grady claimed to have no knowledge of Cindy's whereabouts, and hadn't known that she was being held for ransom by Rossetti, until someone named Ramone called him by using Cindy's phone.

Three witnesses came forth to say that Joe Preston liked to go around claiming to be the owner of a ranch, and often made it sound as if he were a very rich man.

O'Grady's lawyers put forth the theory that Rossetti heard Preston's tales and believed them, then kidnapped his daughter and held her for ransom.

They also contended that their client knew nothing about the insane, "Rescue Mission" that Preston organized, and that the unfortunate men who flew to Vegas with him were duped into believing that Hank O'Grady had sanctioned it.

The whereabouts of Joe Preston and his daughter, Cindy, were unknown, as well as that of Cindy's reputed boyfriend, William Benton.

Mr. Benton and Ms. Preston were only wanted for questioning, but there were warrants out for Joe Preston, and police in both Nevada and Colorado were ready to charge him with numerous crimes.

Meanwhile, New York City crime boss, Johnny R, had vowed to get to the bottom of what happened to his

Uncle Al. He's also pledged that the person responsible for his uncle's death would pay.

When asked what he meant by that last statement, Johnny Rossetti simply grinned.

~

Sara visited Garner in the hospital three days later. She couldn't help but smile when she found four young nurses gathered around the man's bed.

When Garner spotted her, his face lost all trace of pleasure, and he asked the young ladies to leave them alone to talk.

The women did as he asked and each of them graced Sara with a look of either resentment or envy.

"I've come to apologize."

"You're kidding, right?"

Sara hung her head. "I don't expect forgiveness, but I want you to know I'm sorry that I hurt you."

"I shouldn't give you any forgiveness either, but in a way, I have. I've decided not to press charges against you."

"I know. It's why I'm not in jail right now."

She raised her eyes and studied him. "Why are you showing me mercy?"

Garner met her gaze. "I'm not sure myself."

"Whatever the reason, I thank you."

"You need help, Sara, psychiatric help, or this obsession you have for Tanner will eat you alive."

"It's not obsession. The bastard killed the man I love… loved. If our roles were reversed, wouldn't you have risked anything, paid any price to see him suffer?"

"No, not any price and I never would have hurt you. I mean, my God, Sara, you shot me. You shot me, and I nearly died."

Sara wiped at tears, as she spoke in a whisper. "I'm so sorry."

"Get help, please? I didn't know Brian Ames, but I can't imagine he'd want you to ruin your life over his death, not if he loved you half as much as you seemed to have loved him."

Sara took in a big gulp of air and let it out in a sigh.

"Goodbye, Jake, and again, I'm so sorry that I hurt you."

"Get help, Sara, get help."

Sara drifted out of the hospital room with one thought on her mind—finding Tanner.

TWO DAYS LATER, SHE WAS SUMMONED BACK TO THE VEGAS field office where she was presented with a generous offer.

She could stay with the Bureau, in the records department, located in West Virginia. She would no longer be an armed agent, would face little stress, but would have to agree to a year of weekly visits with a Bureau psychiatrist.

She turned the offer down without having to consider it, handed in her credentials, and became a civilian again.

The Bureau had outlived its usefulness to her. She saw that clearly, and she was glad to be free of the restraints and pretense that her position as an agent had forced upon her. She no longer had to feign seeking justice through lawful means when all she really wanted was payback.

There would be no financial difficulties due to job loss either, because Garner had guessed right.

Sara came from money and had inherited a trust fund, thanks to a great-great grandfather who had been an industrialist and amassed a fortune.

Sara didn't need to work and had the money to finance whatever she chose to do with her life.

She had only one desire, or rather, an obsession. Sara wanted to find the man calling himself Tanner and eventually end his life, but only after he paid with agony for killing her love, and he would beg for death before she was through with him. Oh yes, Tanner would beg.

47
THIS WORLD'S A BITCH

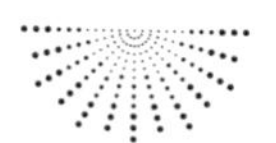

Eleven days after Sara had taken her helicopter ride to search for Tanner in the desert, Billy and Cindy were taking one of their own.

They were in Arizona, at the Grand Canyon, as Cindy fulfilled a dream she had nurtured for years.

They were flying over the South Rim of the canyon but had plans to return the next day and take in the West Rim, along with its famed Skywalk.

The young lovers had taken Tanner's advice and contacted a document forger that Tanner had used in the past. They were scheduled to return to the city of Flagstaff in two days' time to pick up their new IDs and passports, after which they would marry and begin their new lives.

After touring the Grand Canyon, they returned to their motel room. Following a quick swim in the pool, they decided they were hungry, and while Billy showered, Cindy drove across the highway and grabbed food from a drive-thru.

She drove an old Chevy Cavalier that Billy had bought

with cash. Billy hadn't registered the car yet though, he was waiting to do so under his new name.

Cindy returned and was shocked when the door swung open, as she barely touched it with her key card.

She entered, calling Billy's name, and was surprised to hear the shower water still running.

"I'm back, Billy!"

There was no answer. When she looked over at the door, she saw a red handprint above the knob.

"Billy?"

Cindy dropped the bag of food and rushed toward the bathroom, but she halted as a figure emerged from the closet, a figure holding a bloody kitchen knife.

Cindy staggered backwards and stared. "Daddy?"

Joe Preston smiled at his daughter. He looked terrible. Preston had barely eaten or slept in over a week and gray stubble littered his pale face.

He was still wearing the same clothes he'd worn on the evening he'd left Rossetti's property, and the sleeves of his shirt were wet, while the front of it was torn and speckled with blood.

His eyes held a glint of madness and his nose was bloodied and sat crooked, having been broken during a recent struggle; a struggle he had won, thanks to the blade he carried.

"I remembered. You always talked about taking that helicopter ride over the Grand Canyon someday. I remembered, kept watch, and I followed you back here. Did you like it, baby? Was it as much fun as you hoped it would be?"

Cindy gazed at the bathroom door and then at the bloody knife, before sinking to her knees.

"What have you done, Daddy? What have you done?"

"Shh, it'll be okay now, baby. Hank O'Grady, he, he, he

fired me… he fired me on the phone, but, but now, now he'll have to take me back, because I've found you and I'm bringing you home."

Cindy cried out Billy's name in an anguished tone that was more scream than word.

"Biiiilllllly!"

Again, there was no answer, and the room filled with the sound of weeping, as Cindy sank into despair.

48
DOWN TIME

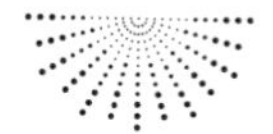

WEEKS LATER

In a private bungalow in the Florida Keys, Tanner watched the young woman he was with rise naked from the bed and pad toward the shower.

She called back over her shoulder, her long, auburn curls framing her face and accentuating her green eyes.

"I'm hungry, baby. Can we eat soon?"

"Yeah, I'll throw some fish on the grill."

"Thank you, lover, and I'll make a salad."

Tanner returned her smile. Her name was Maggie. She was a dental assistant from New Jersey and he'd been shacking up with her for two days after meeting her at a bar in Miami.

Before Maggie, there was Pamela, and Jessica, Lila, and several others.

Tanner was resting, revitalizing himself after his time in prison, while preparing for battle with the Conglomerate, which he knew would come.

He had gone against their wishes and killed Rossetti. They would consider it impertinence and seek to punish him and make an example of him as well.

Tanner had regained the weight he'd lost in prison and was fit and ready for battle. He was an independent contractor and planned to always remain so, but he knew the Conglomerate liked owning things, such as people.

He had always known that someday he and the Conglomerate would clash, and he had prepared for it. In fact, he welcomed it, for in the long run it would prove highly profitable.

Or, they would kill him.

Tanner never feared death. He was death, and he had delivered it to more targets than anyone else in his profession.

TANNER JOINED MAGGIE IN THE SHOWER, AND AFTERWARDS, they emerged cleaned, sated, and with an appetite for food and wine.

Maggie poured the drinks. As she started on the salad, Tanner took out the yellowfin tuna he'd bought from a local fisherman the day before, and removed the cutlets from the old newspaper they were wrapped in.

When Maggie joined him on the patio minutes later, she saw him sitting by the grill, the flame ready, but the fish forgotten and just sitting unwrapped atop the table.

Maggie sat on his lap and ran a hand through his hair as she studied his face.

"Thomas, what's wrong?"

Maggie knew him as Thomas Willis. He'd been using the alias since leaving Vegas.

Tanner looked at her. She was a beautiful woman, and

the feel of her, the weight of woman, it felt comforting to him. Although he was a loner, at that moment, he was glad he wasn't alone.

"Nothing's wrong, why?"

"I don't know. You just had this strange look on your face."

"Is the salad ready?"

"Yes, and hey, tomorrow is my last day of vacation. Why don't we go to Miami?"

"Why not?" Tanner said. A few moments later, he rose to grill the fish.

49
SO CLOSE

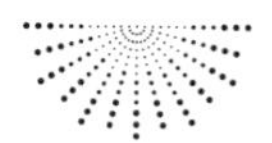

SARA MOVED WITH FURTIVENESS TOWARD TANNER'S bungalow.

It was 2:28 in the morning and she was hoping to catch him asleep and unaware.

It had taken her weeks to track down this alias of Tanner's, weeks of endless searching, detective work, and false leads.

The lock on the patio door proved to be no obstacle, and Sara slid the door open with great care, lest it emit a squeak and warn her prey.

When there was enough room to ease though she did so, and moved with stealth past the living room, down a short hallway, and saw that the door to the bedroom was open.

She stood to the right of the doorway with her back pressed against the wall and listened, while filtering out the lapping of the waves from the beach outside.

The sound of breathing reached her ears, although it was ever so faint, but she could tell it was the soft steady rhythm that accompanied sleep.

She could also tell that it came from two people.

Sara entered the room low, then headed toward the bed in a sideways gait. If Tanner was faking sleep or awakened suddenly, she wanted to give him a narrow target to hit.

Two forms lay atop the bed naked, amid tangled sheets. The woman, Maggie, lay on her back, exposing her breasts. The man was facedown, his right hand hidden beneath the pillow. Sara imagined that it gripped a gun even in sleep.

As she aimed her weapon at the man's torso, she turned on the bedside lamp.

"Wake up and die, Tanner."

Maggie startled awake and gawked at the gun in Sara's hand. "What's going on?" she said, as the man beside her stirred.

Sara jammed the gun into the man's ribs and he jerked awake, turned over, and scrambled back against the wicker headboard while pointing at the gun.

"Shit! What's happening?"

Sara lowered the gun to her side. The man wasn't Tanner.

"Where's Tanner?"

The man looked blank and Maggie shrugged.

"I don't know anyone named Tanner," Maggie said.

Sara sighed in frustration. "Thomas Willis, he's calling himself Thomas Willis."

Maggie swallowed hard. "Oh my God, are you Thomas's wife? I didn't know he was married."

"I'm not his wife. Now, where is he?"

"He left. It was after lunch. He just said he had something to do and left."

"Is he coming back soon?"

"He didn't say, but he did say I could stay here until tomorrow. I didn't break in or anything."

"Who's this?" Sara said, as she looked at the man. He was holding a pillow over his crotch and seemed more frightened than the woman was.

"This is Brad. We met at the bar in the hotel. Thomas was gone, I was alone, and I figured… Thomas said I should make myself at home."

"Do you have any idea where he went or when he'll come back?"

"No, I don't, but he packed up everything and this place is only rented for another two days."

Sara left them without another word and returned outside, where she walked down to the shoreline and gazed up at the stars.

"Goddamn it, Tanner. Where are you?"

50
REVENGE

COLORADO, EIGHTEEN HOURS LATER

Tanner had come across the story when he unwrapped the fish from the old newspaper. The article gave few details, but it was the headline that caught his attention.

MISSING COLORADO TEEN KILLS FATHER, SELF, IN MURDER-SUICIDE, AFTER FATHER SLAYED BOYFRIEND

He figured that Cindy must have used the gun he'd given her, the one he told her she might need someday.

Tanner checked the straps on his backpack, tightened them, and began the hike. The trek took over an hour, and while he walked it, he remembered Cindy and recalled her innocence.

He had shed no tears over Cindy's death.

It was not his way.

His way was different.

His way was final.

When Tanner reached his position, he dropped his gear and removed the small spray can he would need to send a message.

He has to know. I want him to know why.

Tanner walked on to complete his first task, and when he returned, he readied his rifle.

It was an Accuracy International L115A3 sniper rifle. In the hands of an expert, the rifle had an effective range of just over a mile, a limit that Tanner had tested in the past… with success.

He lay flat atop a hill, calculated the elevation in relation to the target, and factored in the wind, which fortunately was quite still, a rarity given that he was firing across an empty field.

Normally, he would take several shots to ensure that he was in range, but he knew he wouldn't miss. No, he wouldn't miss the shot, and it would only take one.

Hank O'Grady slapped his son on the back as he escorted Ricky and his date outside.

It seemed Ricky had recovered from the shock of Cindy's death and moved on to a woman named Amanda.

Hank O'Grady liked Amanda, and it didn't hurt that her father was nearly as rich as he was.

The three of them had dinner together, but the couple had plans, and O'Grady walked them to Ricky's car, a new Mercedes convertible, which Ricky would garage during winter, before switching to his new Chevy Tahoe.

O'Grady saw the couple off with a wave and headed inside.

When he entered his office, he paused in the doorway and puzzled over the writing marring the picture window behind his desk. Large block letters were written there in what looked like red spray paint.

O'Grady moved closer to stand before the desk, where he read the words aloud.

"This is for Cindy," he said, then took note that the dot above the i in the word Cindy resembled a bull's-eye.

He got it. Too late to do anything about it, to duck or even twitch, but O'Grady got it and Tanner saw the knowledge in the man's eyes through his scope.

The bullet passed through the window, entered O'Grady's head and obliterated his features. When it exited his skull, it left little more than a bloody stump behind, and O'Grady's headless corpse tumbled to the floor.

Tanner stood away from the rifle, stepped out of a pair of black coveralls and removed latex gloves.

He would carry these items into the surrounding woods and bury them. It was all evidence now and he would make better time down the mountain without the rifle's weight.

Tanner shrugged into his pack, headed for the trail, and thought of the future, for in the past, in the past lived the dead.

TANNER RETURNS!

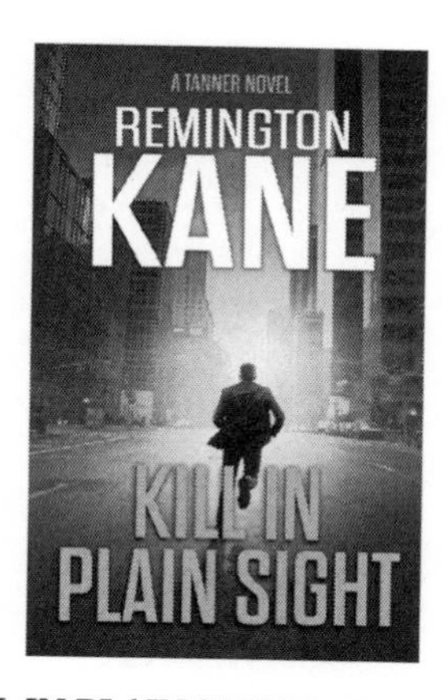

KILL IN PLAIN SIGHT - TANNER 2

AFTERWORD

Thank you,

REMINGTON KANE

JOIN MY INNER CIRCLE

You'll receive FREE books, such as,

SLAY BELLS – A TANNER NOVEL – BOOK 0

TAKEN! ALPHABET SERIES – 26 ORIGINAL TAKEN! TALES

BLUE STEELE - KARMA

Also – Exclusive short stories featuring TANNER, along with other books.

TO BECOME AN INNER CIRCLE MEMBER, GO TO:

http://remingtonkane.com/mailing-list/

ALSO BY REMINGTON KANE

The TANNER Series in order

INEVITABLE I - A Tanner Novel - Book 1

KILL IN PLAIN SIGHT - A Tanner Novel - Book 2

MAKING A KILLING ON WALL STREET - A Tanner Novel - Book 3

THE FIRST ONE TO DIE LOSES - A Tanner Novel - Book 4

THE LIFE & DEATH OF CODY PARKER - A Tanner Novel - Book 5

WAR - A Tanner Novel- A Tanner Novel - Book 6

SUICIDE OR DEATH - A Tanner Novel - Book 7

TWO FOR THE KILL - A Tanner Novel - Book 8

BALLET OF DEATH - A Tanner Novel - Book 9

MORE DANGEROUS THAN MAN - A Tanner Novel - Book 10

TANNER TIMES TWO - A Tanner Novel - Book 11

OCCUPATION: DEATH - A Tanner Novel - Book 12

HELL FOR HIRE - A Tanner Novel - Book 13

A HOME TO DIE FOR - A Tanner Novel - Book 14

FIRE WITH FIRE - A Tanner Novel - Book 15

TO KILL A KILLER - A Tanner Novel - Book 16

WHITE HELL – A Tanner Novel - Book 17

MANHATTAN HIT MAN – A Tanner Novel - Book 18

ONE HUNDRED YEARS OF TANNER – A Tanner Novel -

Book 19

REVELATIONS - A Tanner Novel - Book 20

THE SPY GAME - A Tanner Novel - Book 21

A VICTIM OF CIRCUMSTANCE - A Tanner Novel - Book 22

A MAN OF RESPECT - A Tanner Novel - Book 23

THE MAN, THE MYTH - A Tanner Novel - Book 24

ALL-OUT WAR - A Tanner Novel - Book 25

THE REAL DEAL - A Tanner Novel - Book 26

WAR ZONE - A Tanner Novel - Book 27

ULTIMATE ASSASSIN - A Tanner Novel - Book 28

KNIGHT TIME - A Tanner Novel - Book 29

PROTECTOR - A Tanner Novel - Book 30

BULLETS BEFORE BREAKFAST - A Tanner Novel - Book 31

VENGEANCE - A Tanner Novel - Book 32

TARGET: TANNER - A Tanner Novel - Book 33

BLACK SHEEP - A Tanner Novel - Book 34

FLESH AND BLOOD - A Tanner Novel - Book 35

NEVER SEE IT COMING - A Tanner Novel - Book 36

MISSING - A Tanner Novel - Book 37

CONTENDER - A Tanner Novel - Book 38

TO SERVE AND PROTECT - A Tanner Novel - Book 39

STALKING HORSE - A Tanner Novel - Book 40

THE EVIL OF TWO LESSERS - A Tanner Novel - Book 41

SINS OF THE FATHER AND MOTHER - A Tanner Novel - Book 42

SOULLESS - A Tanner Novel - Book 43

The Young Guns Series in order

YOUNG GUNS

YOUNG GUNS 2 - SMOKE & MIRRORS

YOUNG GUNS 3 - BEYOND LIMITS

YOUNG GUNS 4 - RYKER'S RAIDERS

YOUNG GUNS 5 - ULTIMATE TRAINING

YOUNG GUNS 6 - CONTRACT TO KILL

YOUNG GUNS 7 - FIRST LOVE

YOUNG GUNS 8 - THE END OF THE BEGINNING

A Tanner Series in order

TANNER: YEAR ONE

TANNER: YEAR TWO

TANNER: YEAR THREE

TANNER: YEAR FOUR

TANNER: YEAR FIVE

The TAKEN! Series in order

TAKEN! - LOVE CONQUERS ALL - Book 1

TAKEN! - SECRETS & LIES - Book 2

TAKEN! - STALKER - Book 3

TAKEN! - BREAKOUT! - Book 4

TAKEN! - THE THIRTY-NINE - Book 5

TAKEN! - KIDNAPPING THE DEVIL - Book 6

TAKEN! - HIT SQUAD - Book 7

TAKEN! - MASQUERADE - Book 8

TAKEN! - SERIOUS BUSINESS - Book 9

TAKEN! - THE COUPLE THAT SLAYS TOGETHER - Book 10

TAKEN! - PUT ASUNDER - Book 11

TAKEN! - LIKE BOND, ONLY BETTER - Book 12

TAKEN! - MEDIEVAL - Book 13

TAKEN! - RISEN! - Book 14

TAKEN! - VACATION - Book 15

TAKEN! - MICHAEL - Book 16

TAKEN! - BEDEVILED - Book 17

TAKEN! - INTENTIONAL ACTS OF VIOLENCE - Book 18

TAKEN! - THE KING OF KILLERS – Book 19

TAKEN! - NO MORE MR. NICE GUY - Book 20 & the Series Finale

The MR. WHITE Series

PAST IMPERFECT - MR. WHITE - Book 1

HUNTED - MR. WHITE - Book 2

The BLUE STEELE Series in order

BLUE STEELE - BOUNTY HUNTER- Book 1

BLUE STEELE - BROKEN- Book 2

BLUE STEELE - VENGEANCE- Book 3

BLUE STEELE - THAT WHICH DOESN'T KILL ME- Book 4

BLUE STEELE - ON THE HUNT- Book 5

BLUE STEELE - PAST SINS - Book 6

BLUE STEELE - DADDY'S GIRL - Book 7 & the Series Finale

The CALIBER DETECTIVE AGENCY Series in order

CALIBER DETECTIVE AGENCY - GENERATIONS- Book 1

CALIBER DETECTIVE AGENCY - TEMPTATION- Book 2

CALIBER DETECTIVE AGENCY - A RANSOM PAID IN BLOOD- Book 3

CALIBER DETECTIVE AGENCY - MISSING- Book 4

CALIBER DETECTIVE AGENCY - DECEPTION- Book 5

CALIBER DETECTIVE AGENCY - CRUCIBLE- Book 6

CALIBER DETECTIVE AGENCY – LEGENDARY – Book 7

CALIBER DETECTIVE AGENCY – WE ARE GATHERED HERE TODAY - Book 8

CALIBER DETECTIVE AGENCY - MEANS, MOTIVE, and OPPORTUNITY - Book 9 & the Series Finale

THE TAKEN!/TANNER Series in order

THE CONTRACT: KILL JESSICA WHITE - Taken!/Tanner - Book 1

UNFINISHED BUSINESS – Taken!/Tanner – Book 2

THE ABDUCTION OF THOMAS LAWSON - Taken!/Tanner – Book 3

PREDATOR - Taken!/Tanner - Book 4

DETECTIVE PIERCE Series in order

MONSTERS - A Detective Pierce Novel - Book 1

DEMONS - A Detective Pierce Novel - Book 2

ANGELS - A Detective Pierce Novel - Book 3

THE OCEAN BEACH ISLAND Series in order

THE MANY AND THE ONE - Book 1

SINS & SECOND CHANES - Book 2

DRY ADULTERY, WET AMBITION -Book 3

OF TONGUE AND PEN - Book 4

ALL GOOD THINGS… - Book 5

LITTLE WHITE SINS - Book 6

THE LIGHT OF DARKNESS - Book 7

STERN ISLAND - Book 8 & the Series Finale

THE REVENGE Series in order

JOHNNY REVENGE - The Revenge Series - Book 1

THE APPOINTMENT KILLER - The Revenge Series - Book 2

AN I FOR AN I - The Revenge Series - Book 3

ALSO

THE EFFECT: Reality is changing!

THE FIX-IT MAN: A Tale of True Love and Revenge

DOUBLE OR NOTHING

PARKER & KNIGHT

REDEMPTION: Someone's taken her

DESOLATION LAKE

TIME TRAVEL TALES & OTHER SHORT STORIES

YEAR ZERO PUBLISHING

Created with Vellum

Printed in Great Britain
by Amazon